BRAM STOKER'S
DRACULA

RETOLD BY MICHAEL BURGAN

illustrated by José Alfonso Ocampo Ruiz
cover color by Benny Fuentes
interior color by Protobunker Studio

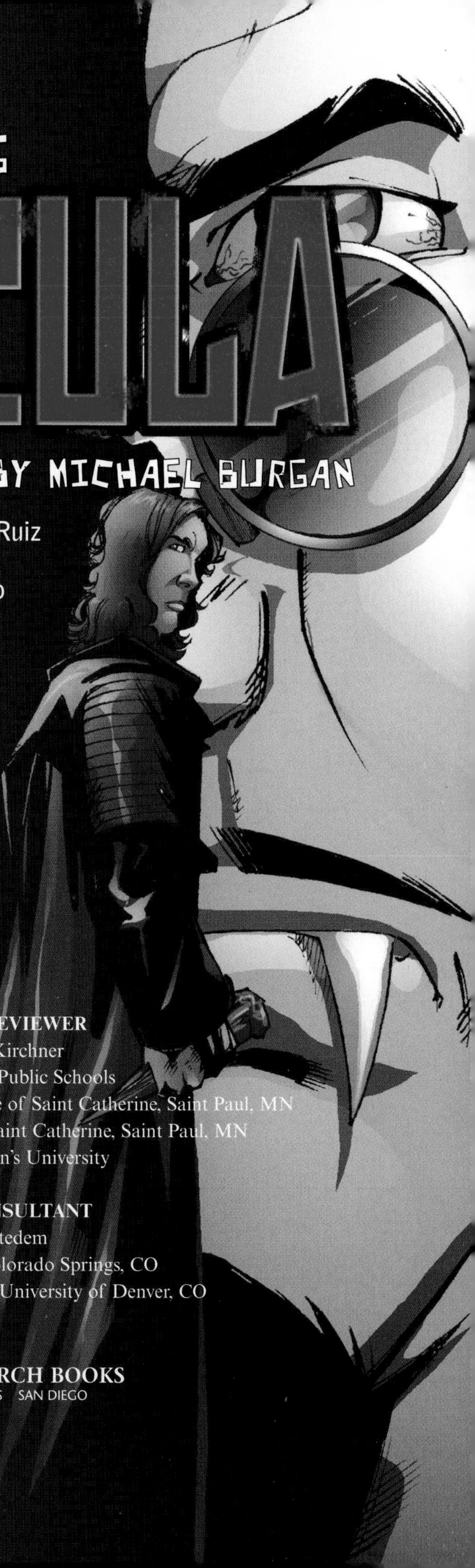

LIBRARIAN REVIEWER
Julie Potvin Kirchner
Educator, Wayzata Public Schools
BA in Elementary Education, The College of Saint Catherine, Saint Paul, MN
MA in Education, The College of Saint Catherine, Saint Paul, MN
MLS, Texas Woman's University

READING CONSULTANT
Elizabeth Stedem
Educator/Consultant, Colorado Springs, CO
MA in Elementary Education, University of Denver, CO

STONE ARCH BOOKS
MINNEAPOLIS SAN DIEGO

Graphic Revolve is published by Stone Arch Books
151 Good Counsel Drive, P.O. Box 669
Mankato, Minnesota 56002
www.stonearchbooks.com

Library of Congress Cataloging-in-Publication Data
Burgan, Michael.
Dracula / Bram Stoker (retold by Michael Burgan); illustrated by José Alfonso Ocampo Ruiz.
p. cm. — (Graphic Revolve)
ISBN 978-1-4342-0448-6 (library binding)
ISBN 978-1-4342-0498-1 (paperback)
1. Graphic novels. I. Ocampo Ruiz, José Alfonso. II. Stoker, Bram, 1847–1912. Dracula. III. Title.
PN6727.B855D73 2008
741.5'973—dc22 2007030805

Summary: On a business trip to Transylvania, Jonathan Harker stays at an eerie castle owned by a man named Count Dracula. When strange things start to happen, Harker investigates and finds the count sleeping in a coffin! Harker isn't safe, and when the count escapes to London, neither are his friends.

Art Director: Heather Kindseth
Graphic Designer: Kay Fraser

1 2 3 4 5 6 13 12 11 10 09 08

Printed in the United States of America

TABLE OF CONTENTS

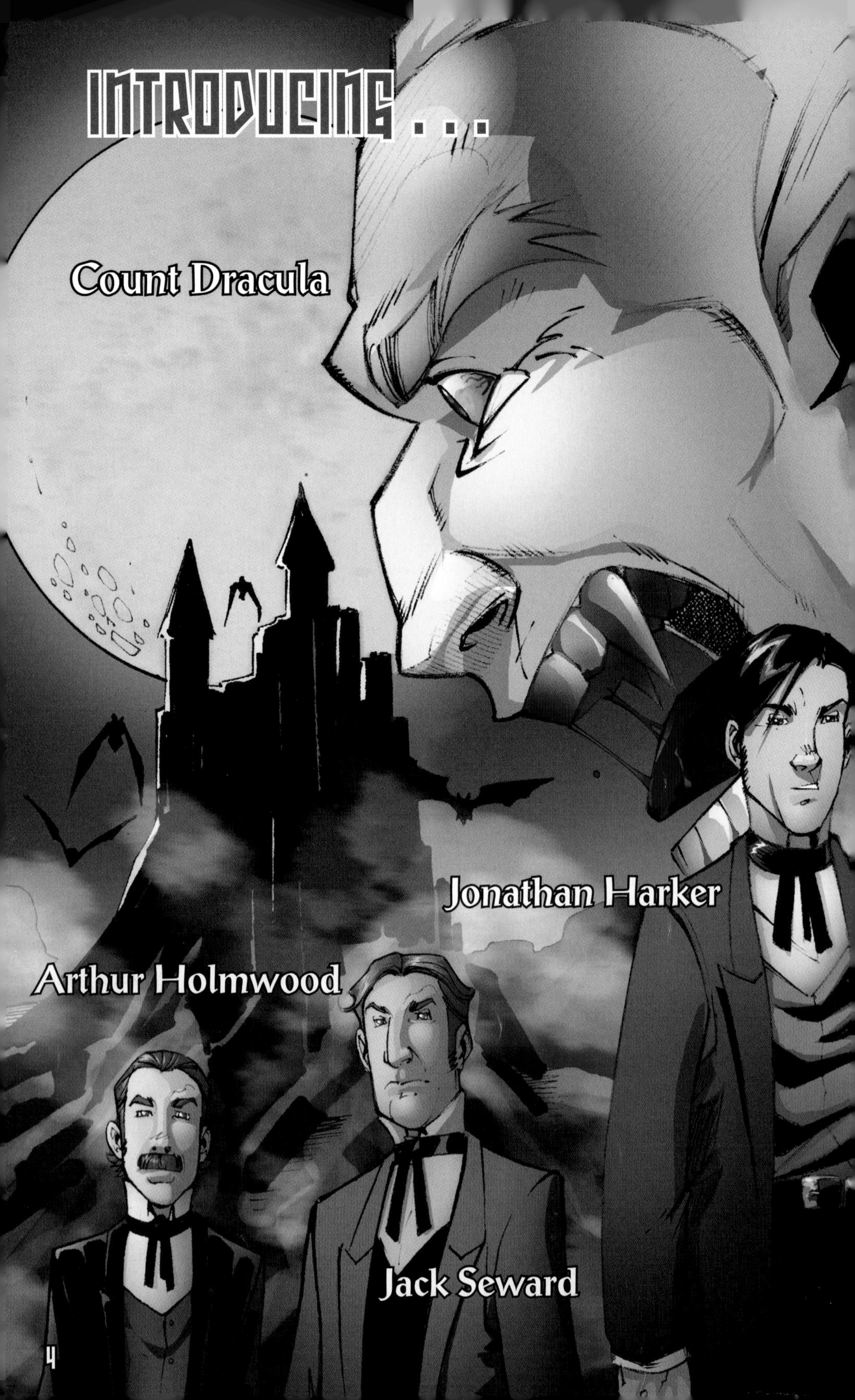

INTRODUCING . . .
Count Dracula
Jonathan Harker
Arthur Holmwood
Jack Seward

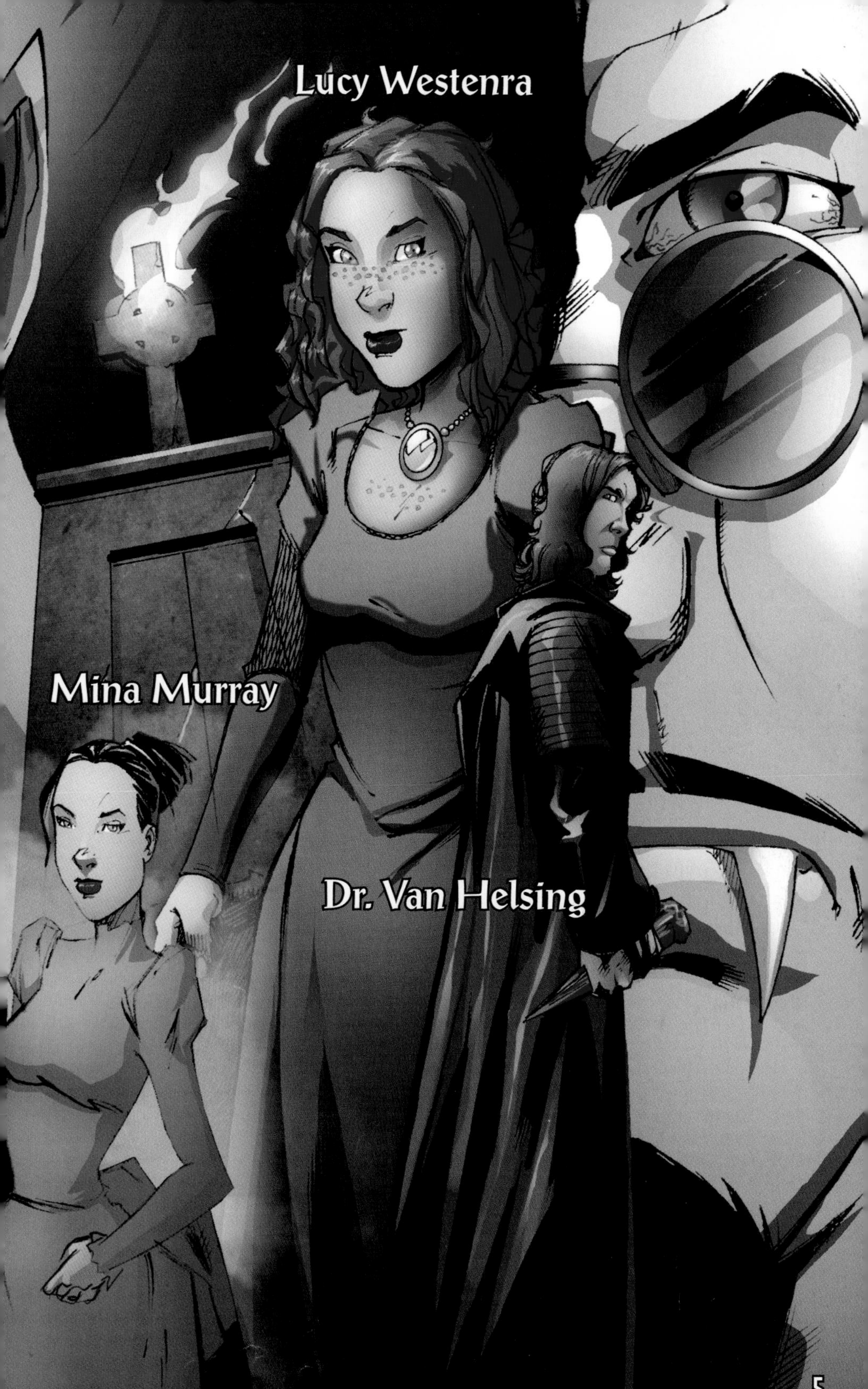
Lucy Westenra
Mina Murray
Dr. Van Helsing

CHAPTER 1: THE CASTLE OF HORROR

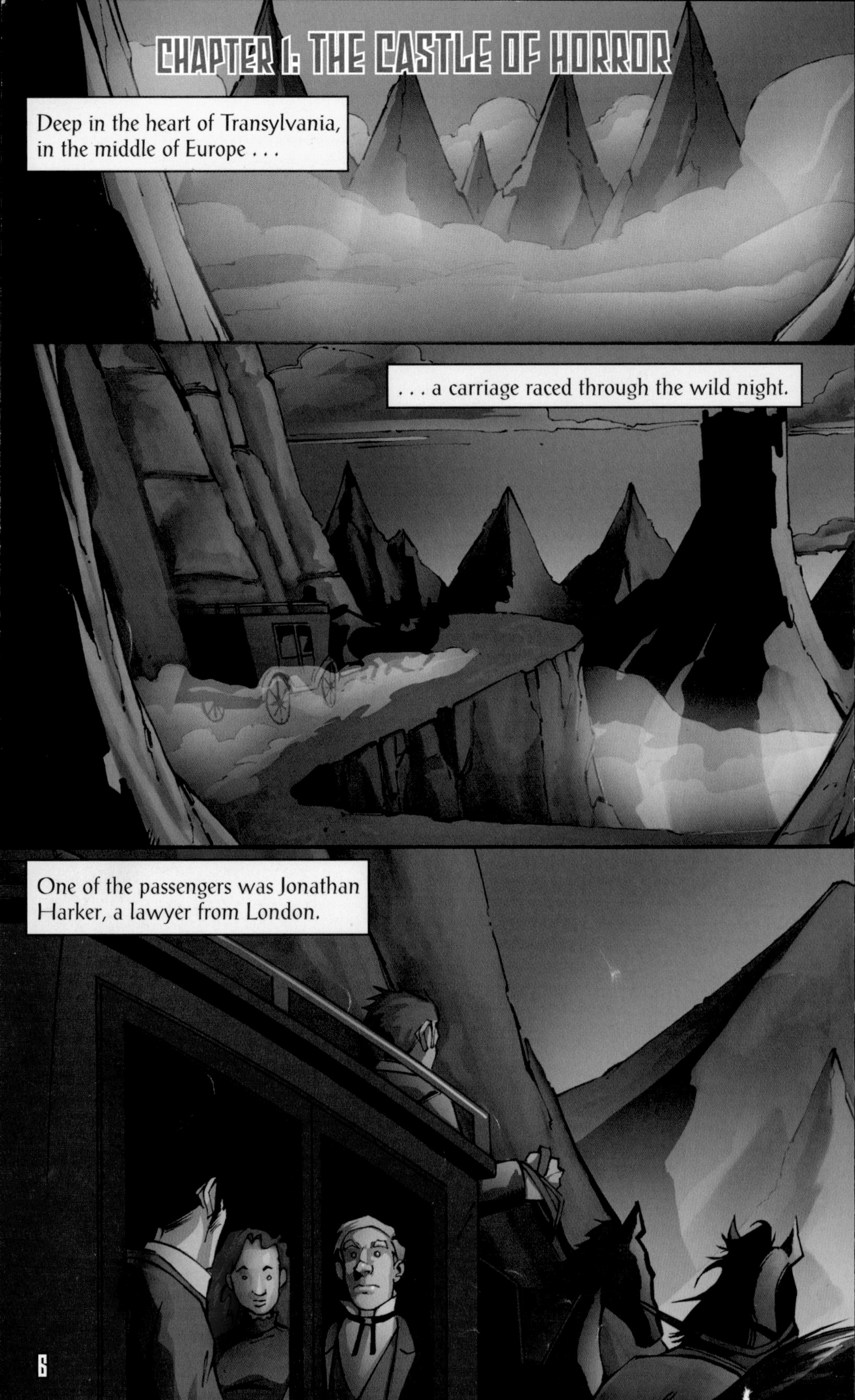
Deep in the heart of Transylvania, in the middle of Europe . . .
. . . a carriage raced through the wild night.
One of the passengers was Jonathan Harker, a lawyer from London.

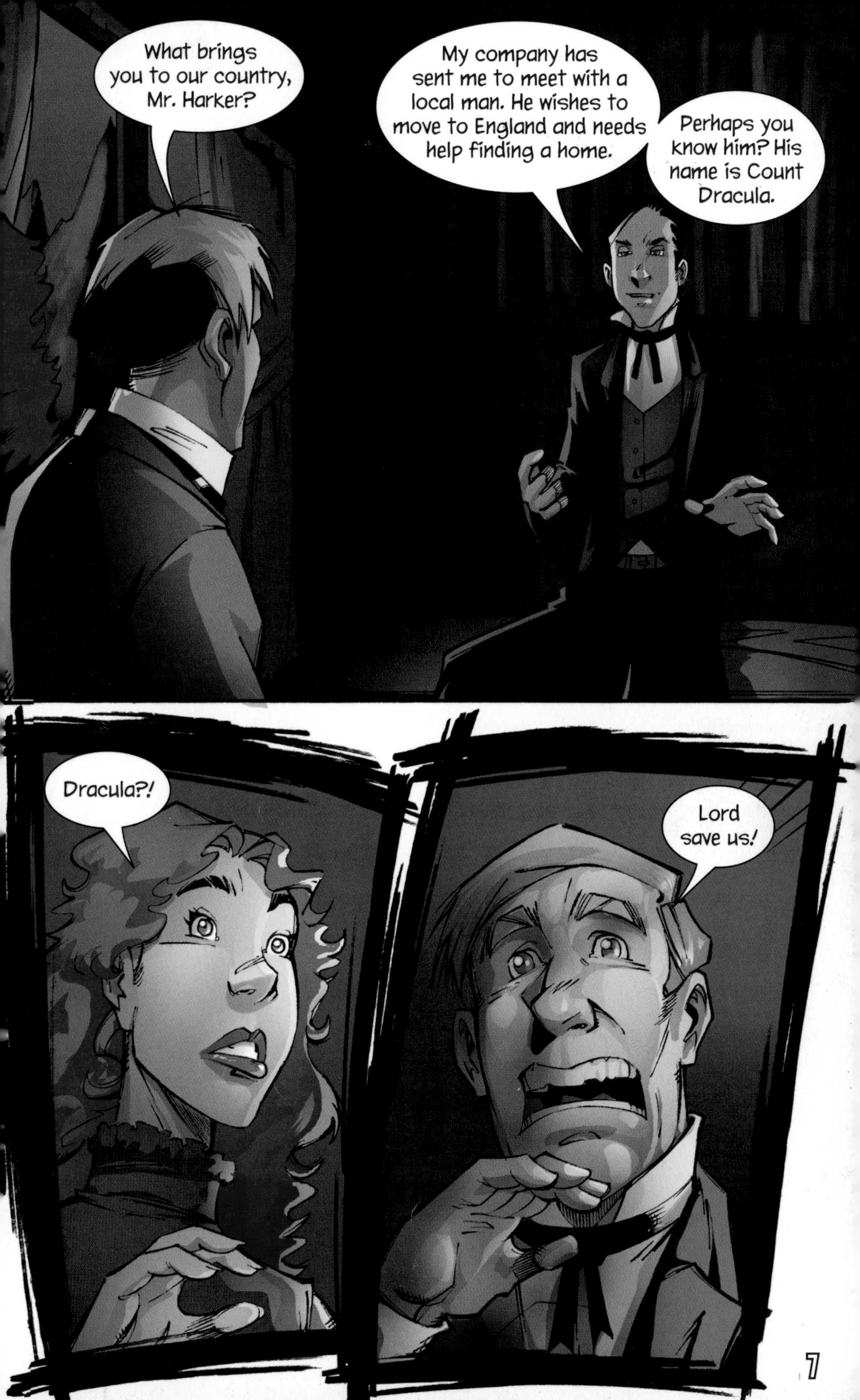
What brings you to our country, Mr. Harker?
My company has sent me to meet with a local man. He wishes to move to England and needs help finding a home.
Perhaps you know him? His name is Count Dracula.
Dracula?!
Lord save us!

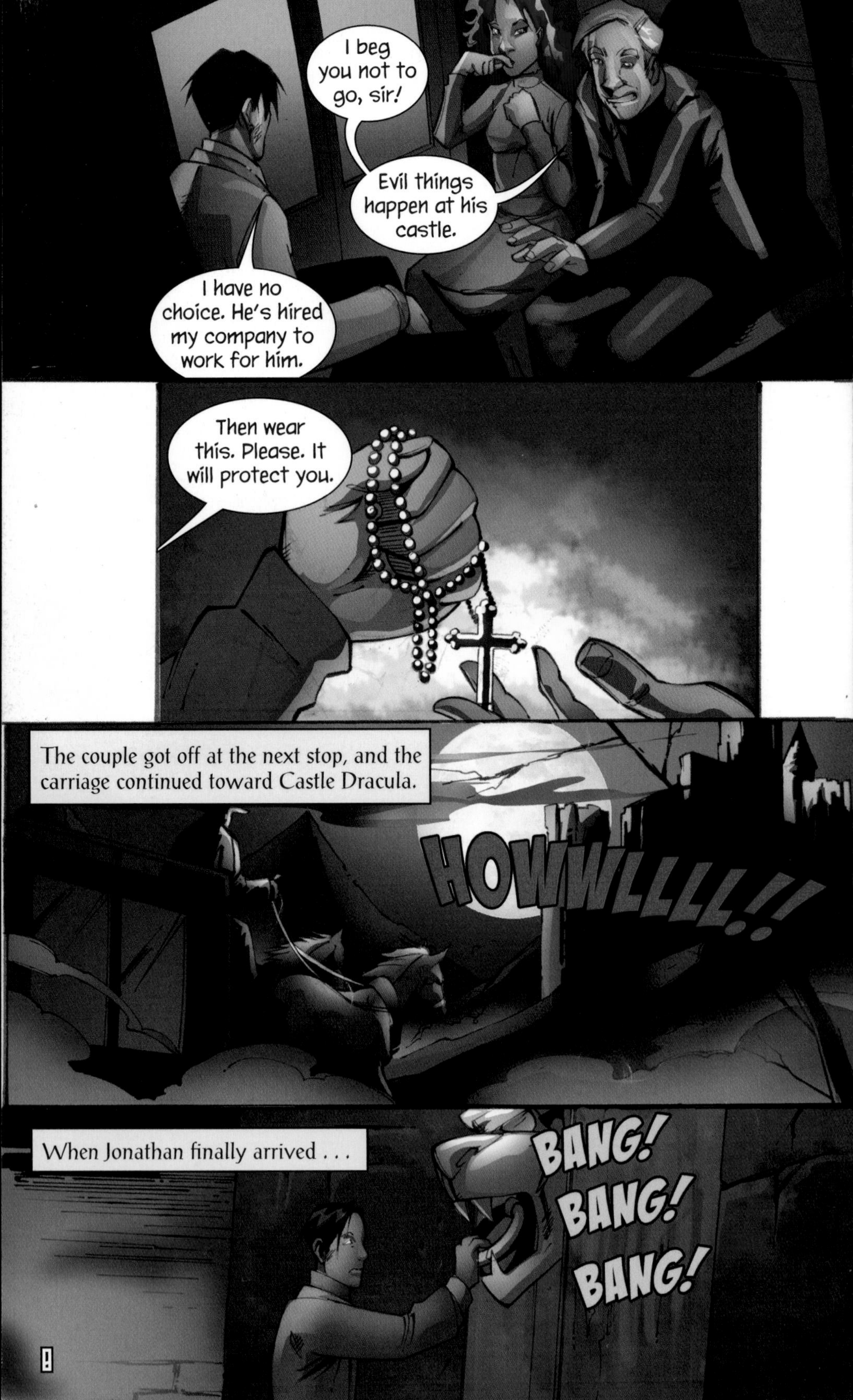
I beg you not to go, sir!
Evil things happen at his castle.
I have no choice. He's hired my company to work for him.
Then wear this. Please. It will protect you.
The couple got off at the next stop, and the carriage continued toward Castle Dracula.
HOWWLLLL!!
When Jonathan finally arrived . . .
BANG!
BANG!
BANG!

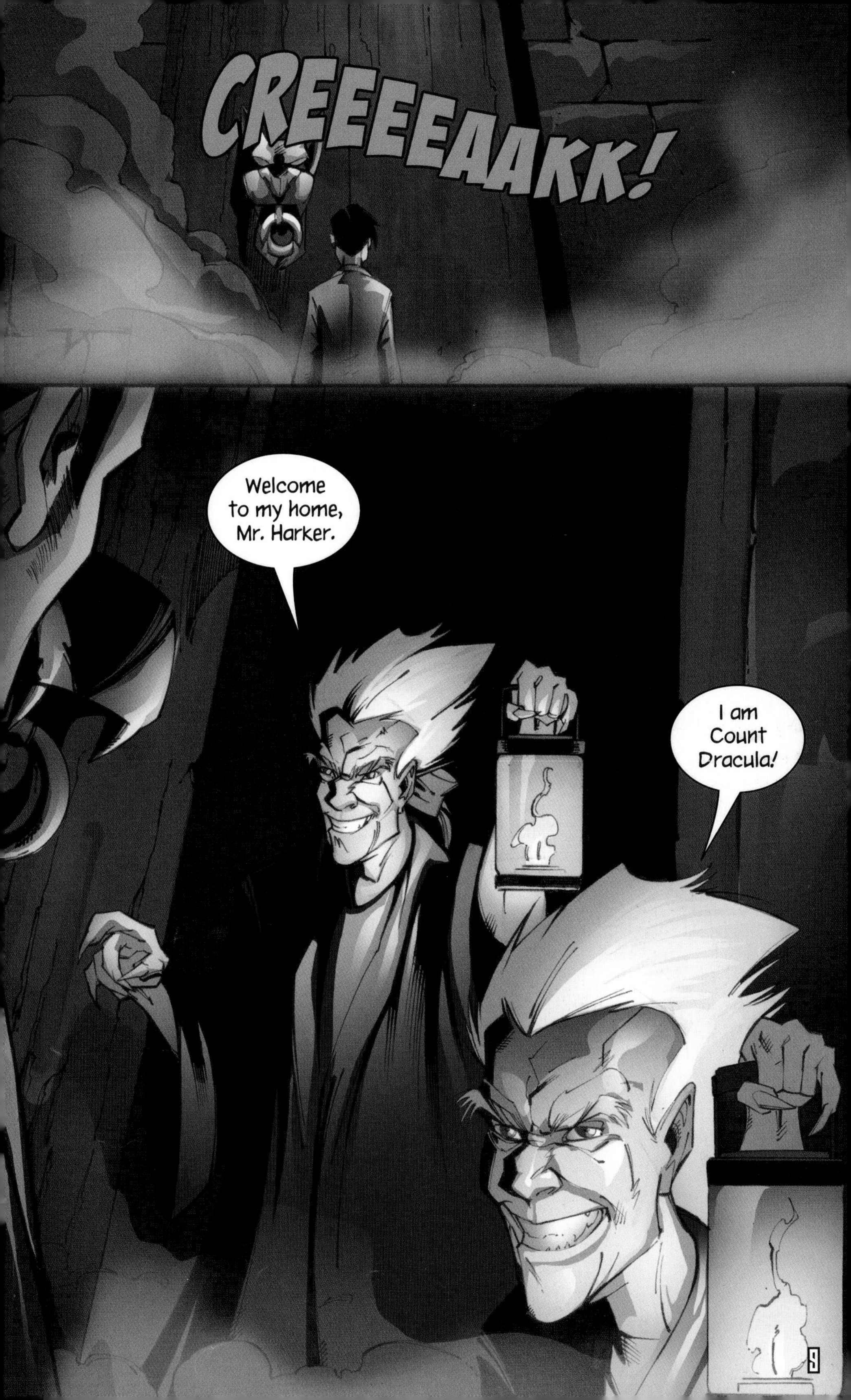
CREEEEAAKK!
Welcome to my home, Mr. Harker.
I am Count Dracula!

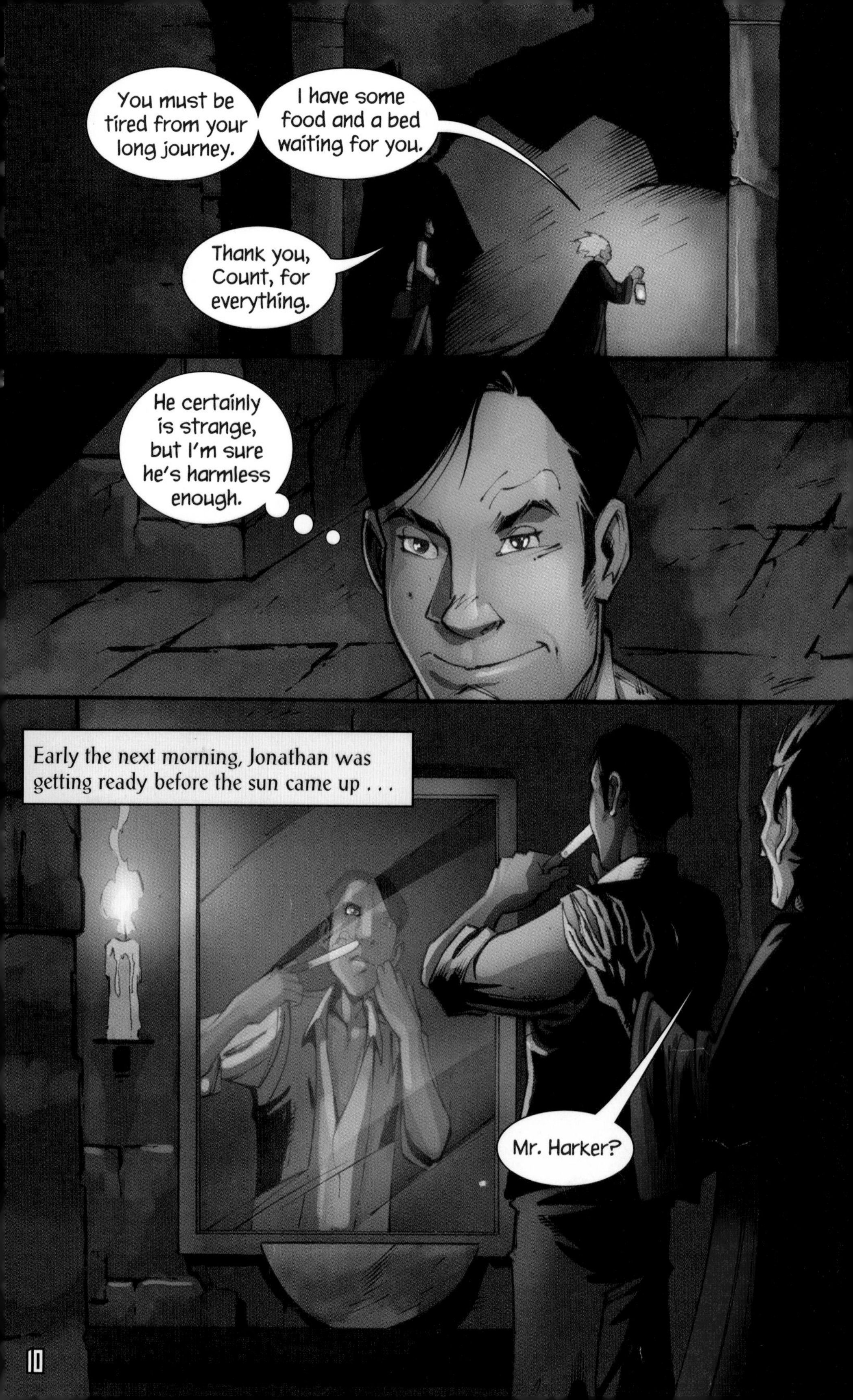
You must be tired from your long journey.
I have some food and a bed waiting for you.
Thank you, Count, for everything.
He certainly is strange, but I'm sure he's harmless enough.
Early the next morning, Jonathan was getting ready before the sun came up . . .
Mr. Harker?

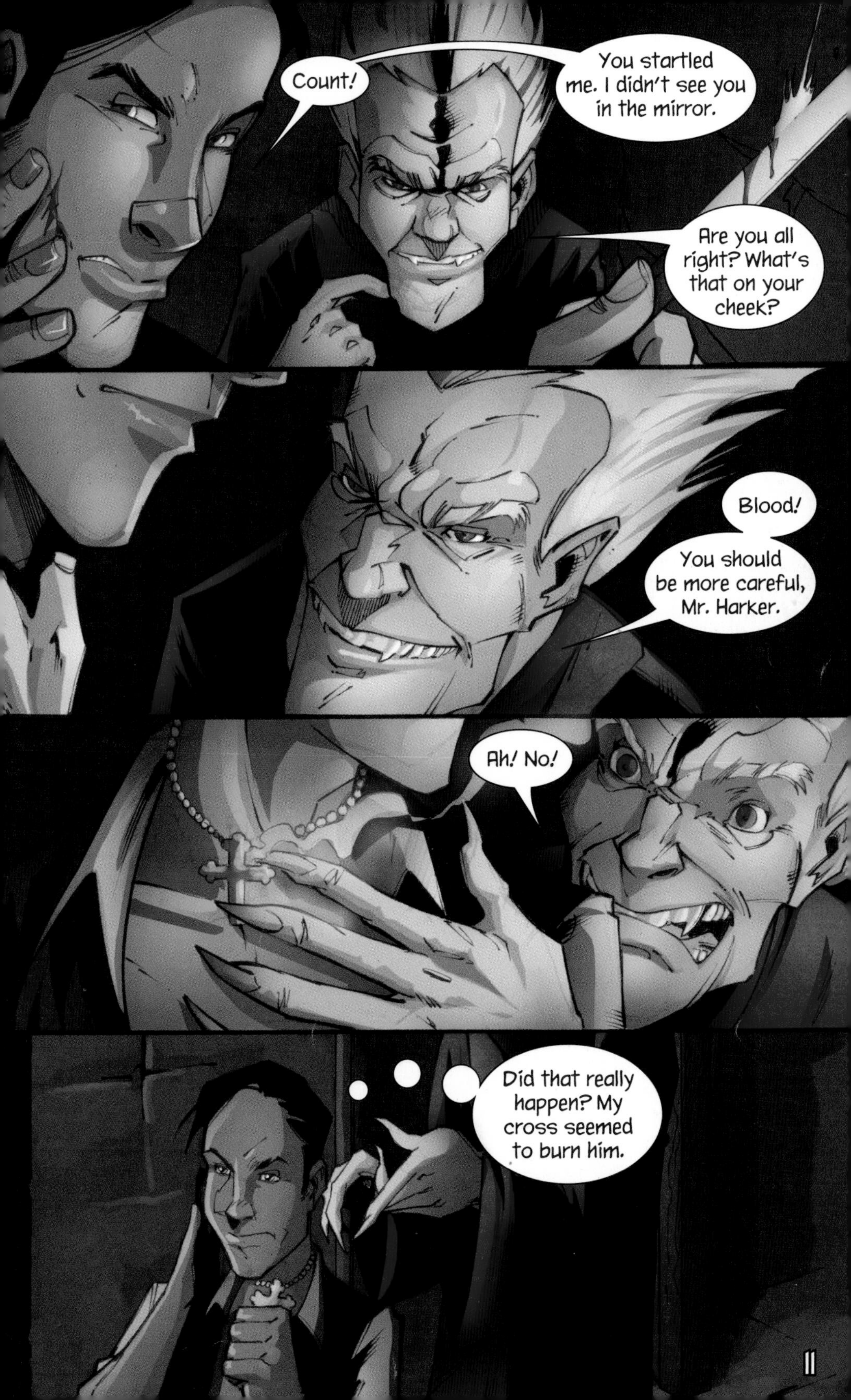
Count!
You startled me. I didn't see you in the mirror.
Are you all right? What's that on your cheek?
Blood!
You should be more careful, Mr. Harker.
Ah! No!
Did that really happen? My cross seemed to burn him.

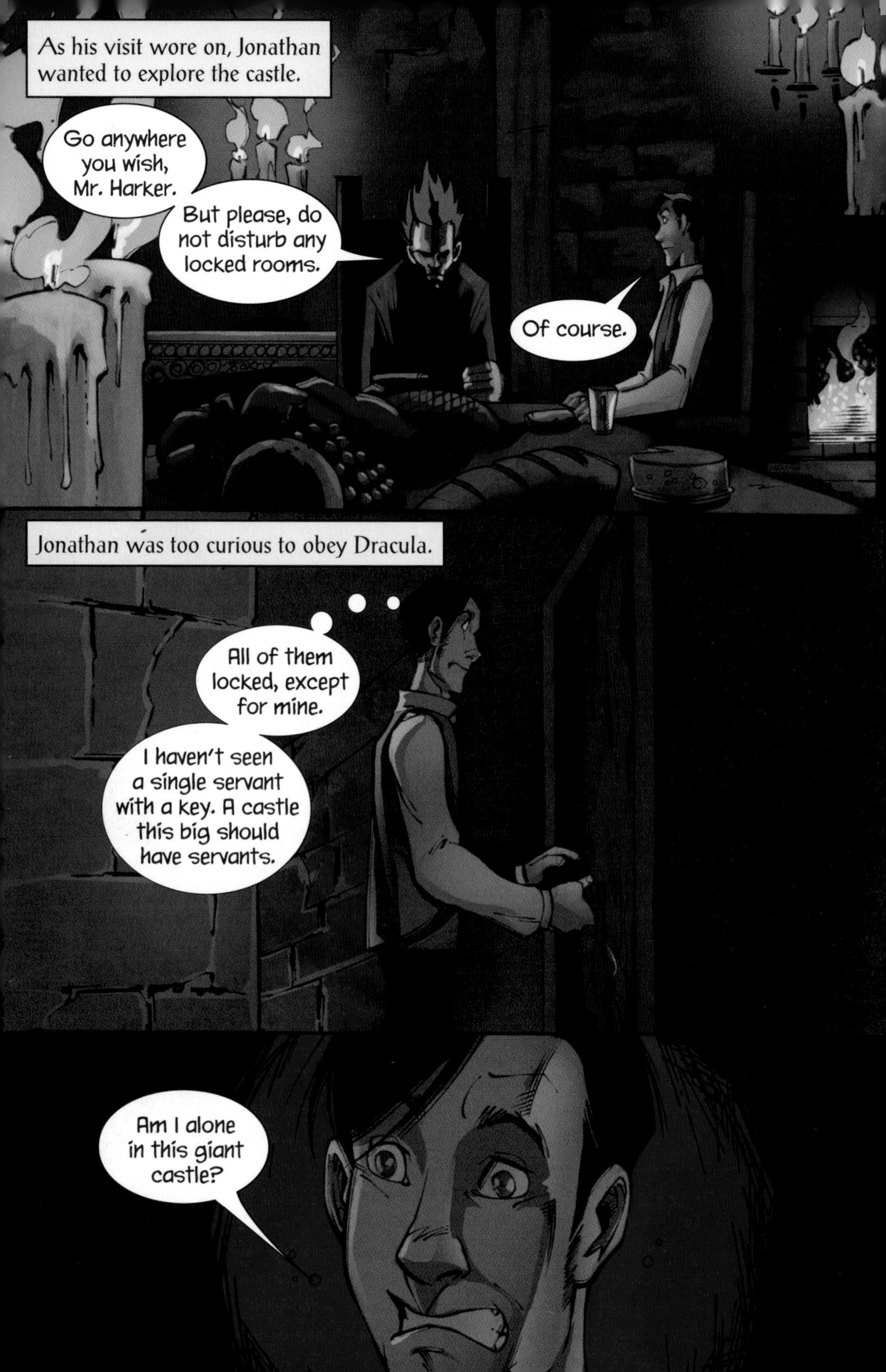
As his visit wore on, Jonathan wanted to explore the castle.
Go anywhere you wish, Mr. Harker.
But please, do not disturb any locked rooms.
Of course.
Jonathan was too curious to obey Dracula.
All of them locked, except for mine.
I haven't seen a single servant with a key. A castle this big should have servants.
Am I alone in this giant castle?

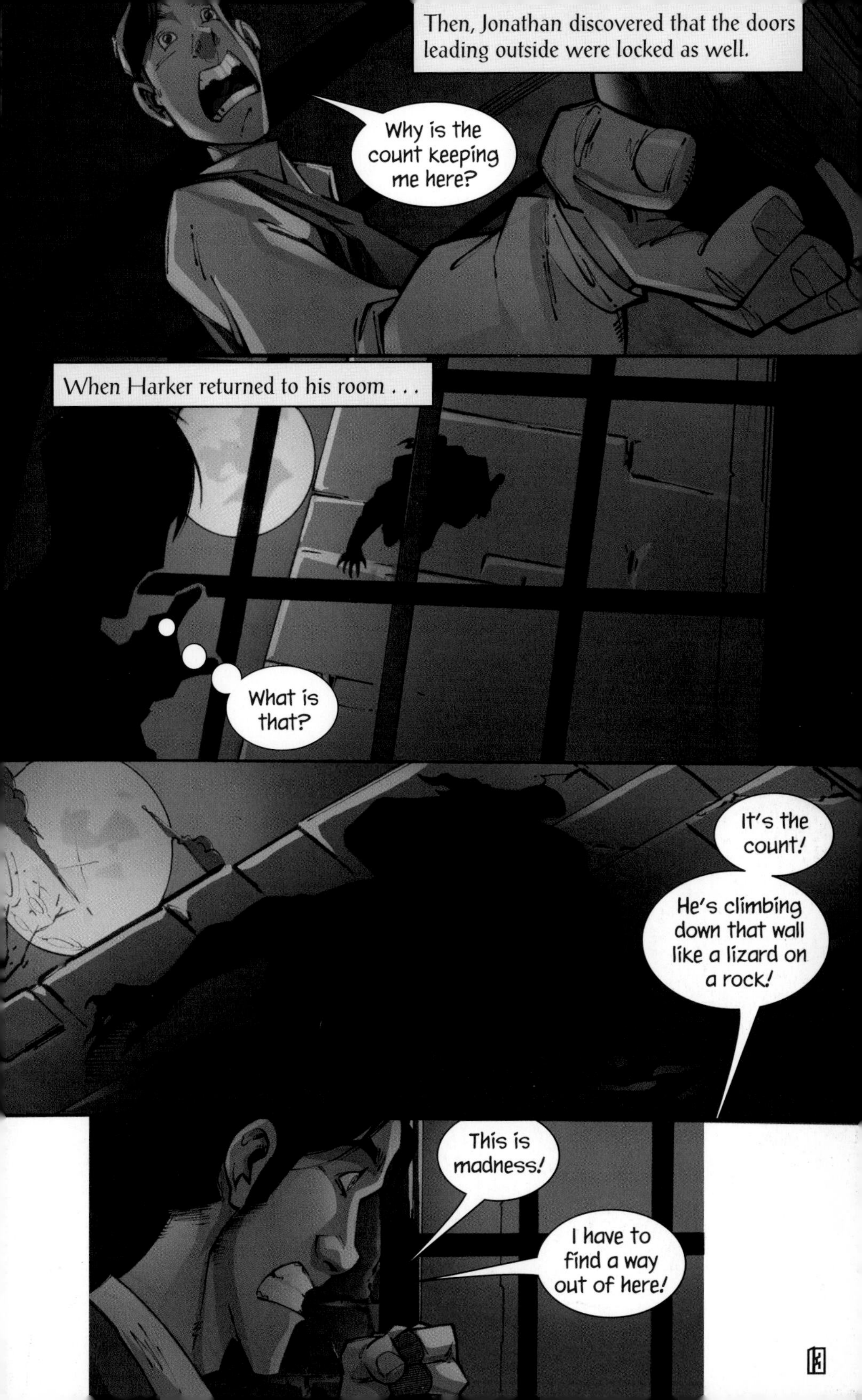
Then, Jonathan discovered that the doors leading outside were locked as well.
Why is the count keeping me here?
When Harker returned to his room . . .
What is that?
It's the count!
He's climbing down that wall like a lizard on a rock!
This is madness!
I have to find a way out of here!

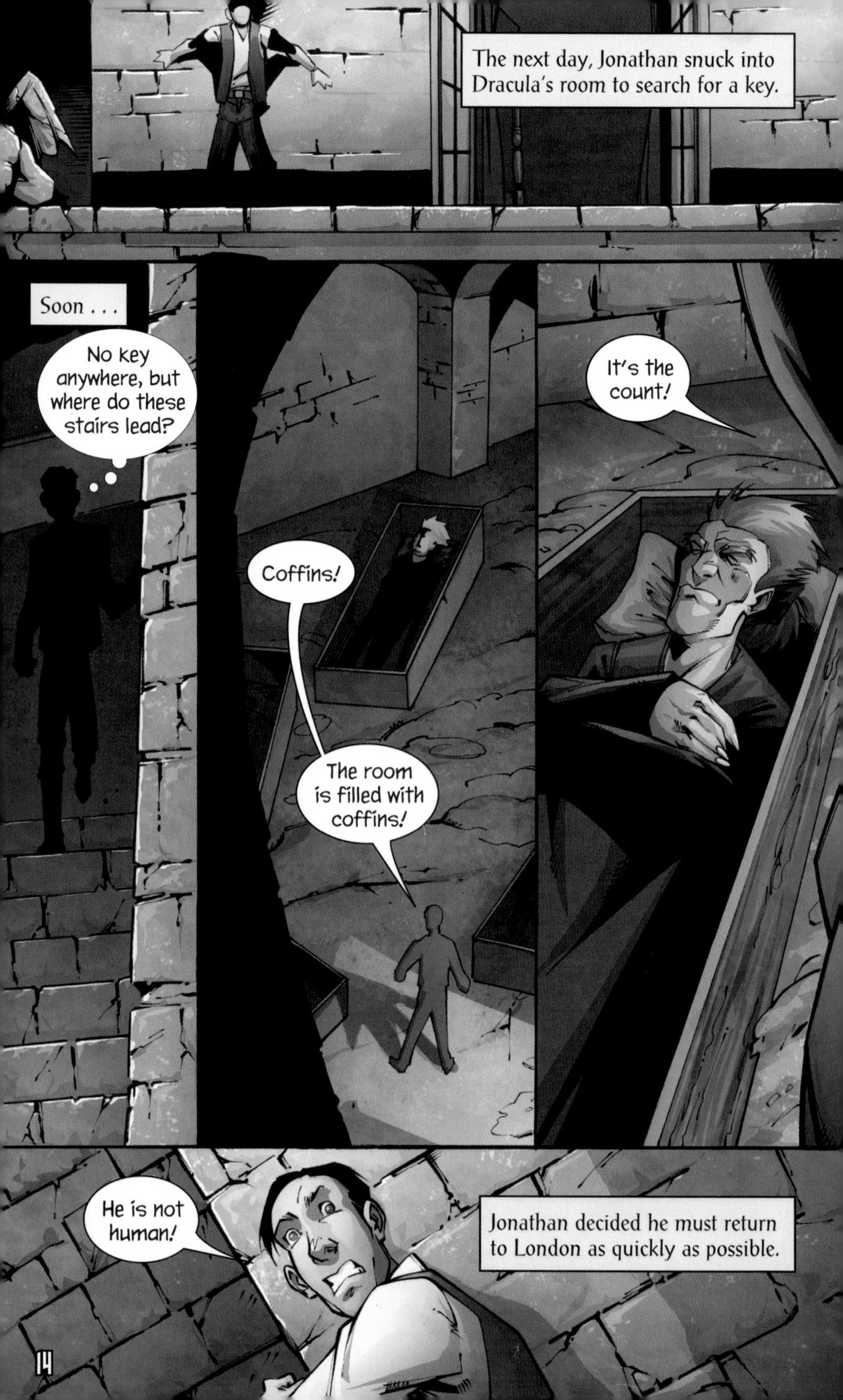
The next day, Jonathan snuck into Dracula's room to search for a key.
Soon . . .
No key anywhere, but where do these stairs lead?
Coffins!
The room is filled with coffins!
It's the count!
He is not human!
Jonathan decided he must return to London as quickly as possible.

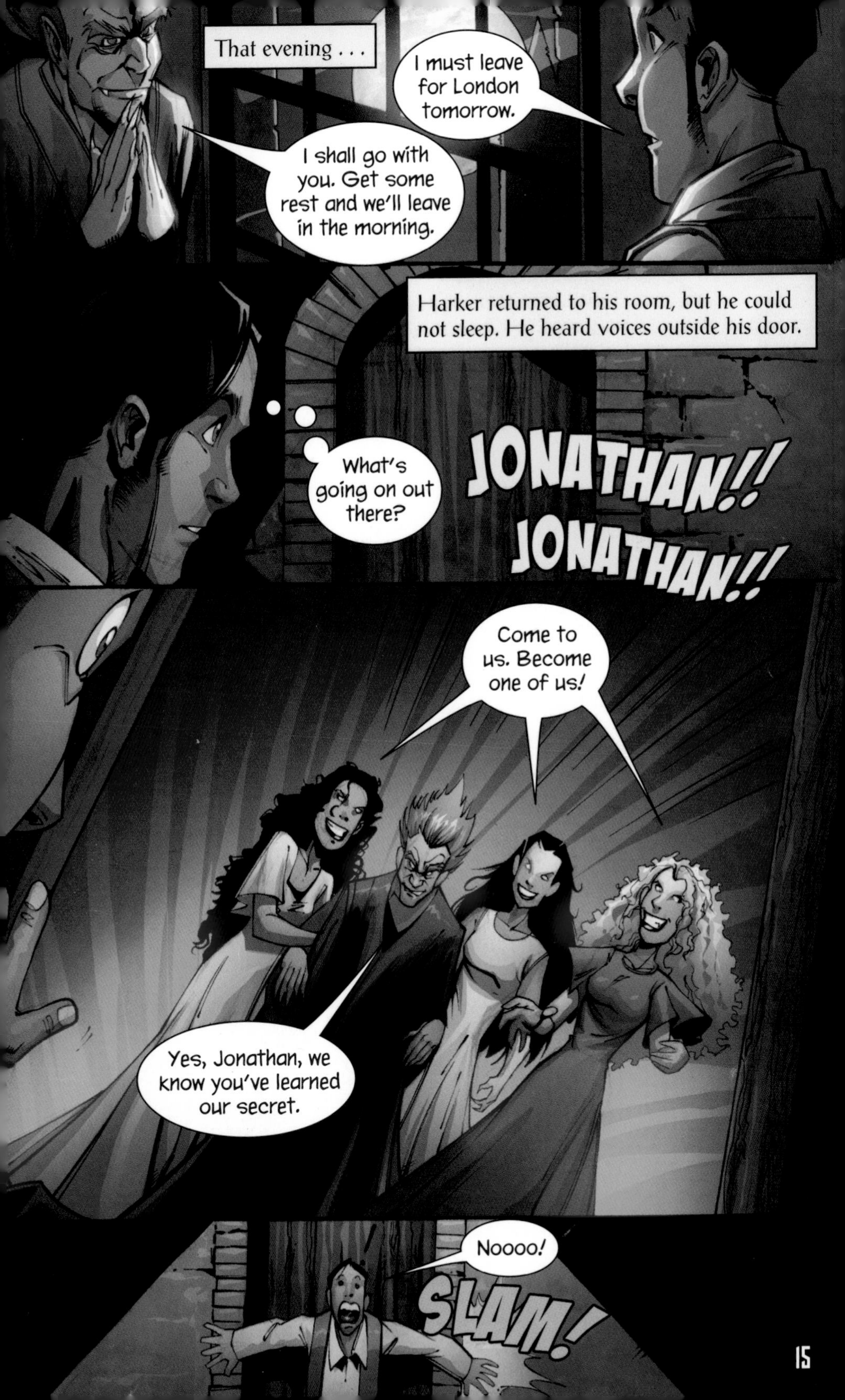
That evening . . .
I must leave for London tomorrow.
I shall go with you. Get some rest and we'll leave in the morning.
Harker returned to his room, but he could not sleep. He heard voices outside his door.
What's going on out there?
JONATHAN!!
JONATHAN!!
Come to us. Become one of us!
Yes, Jonathan, we know you've learned our secret.
Noooo!
SLAM!

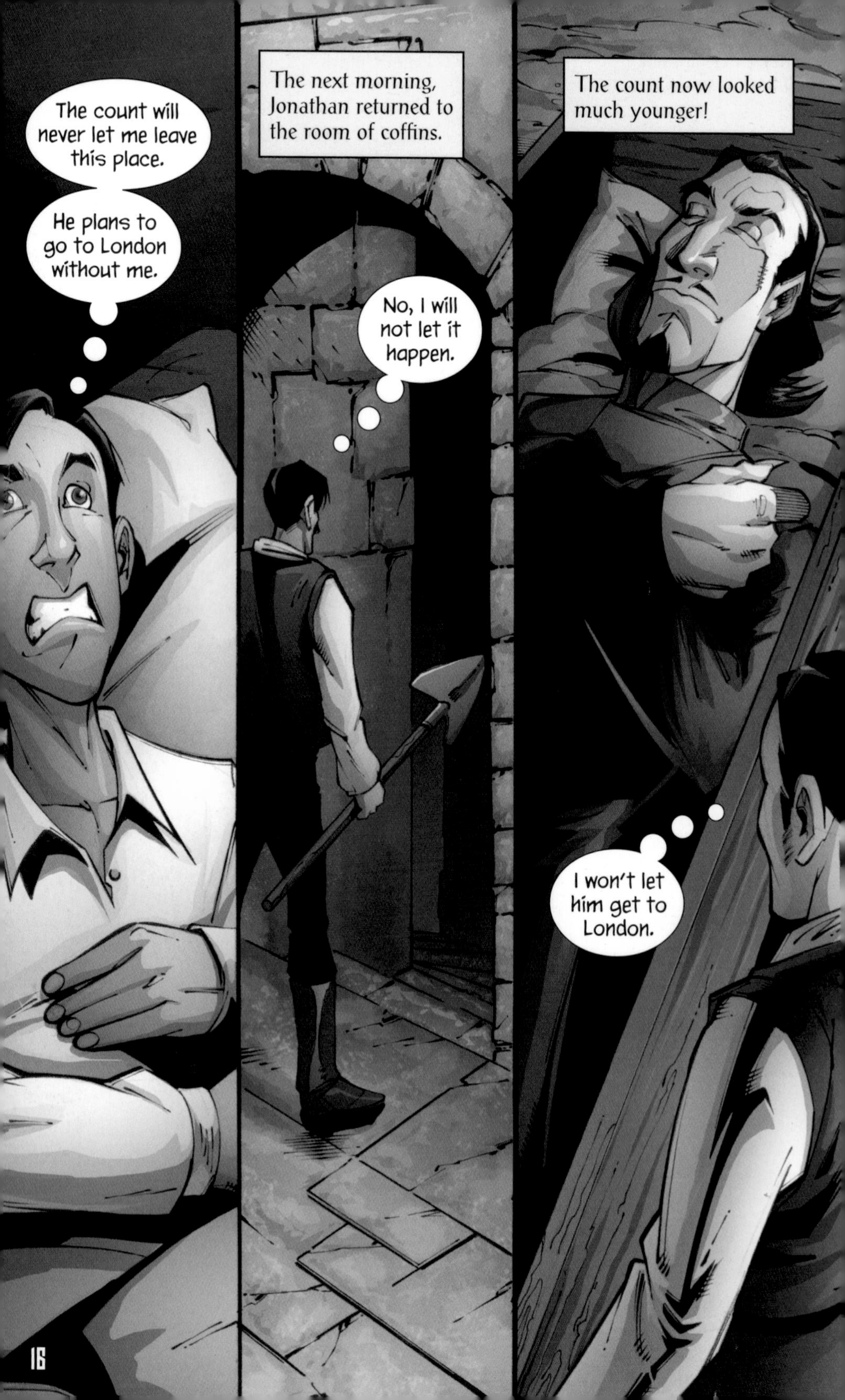
The count will never let me leave this place.
He plans to go to London without me.
The next morning, Jonathan returned to the room of coffins.
No, I will not let it happen.
The count now looked much younger!
I won't let him get to London.

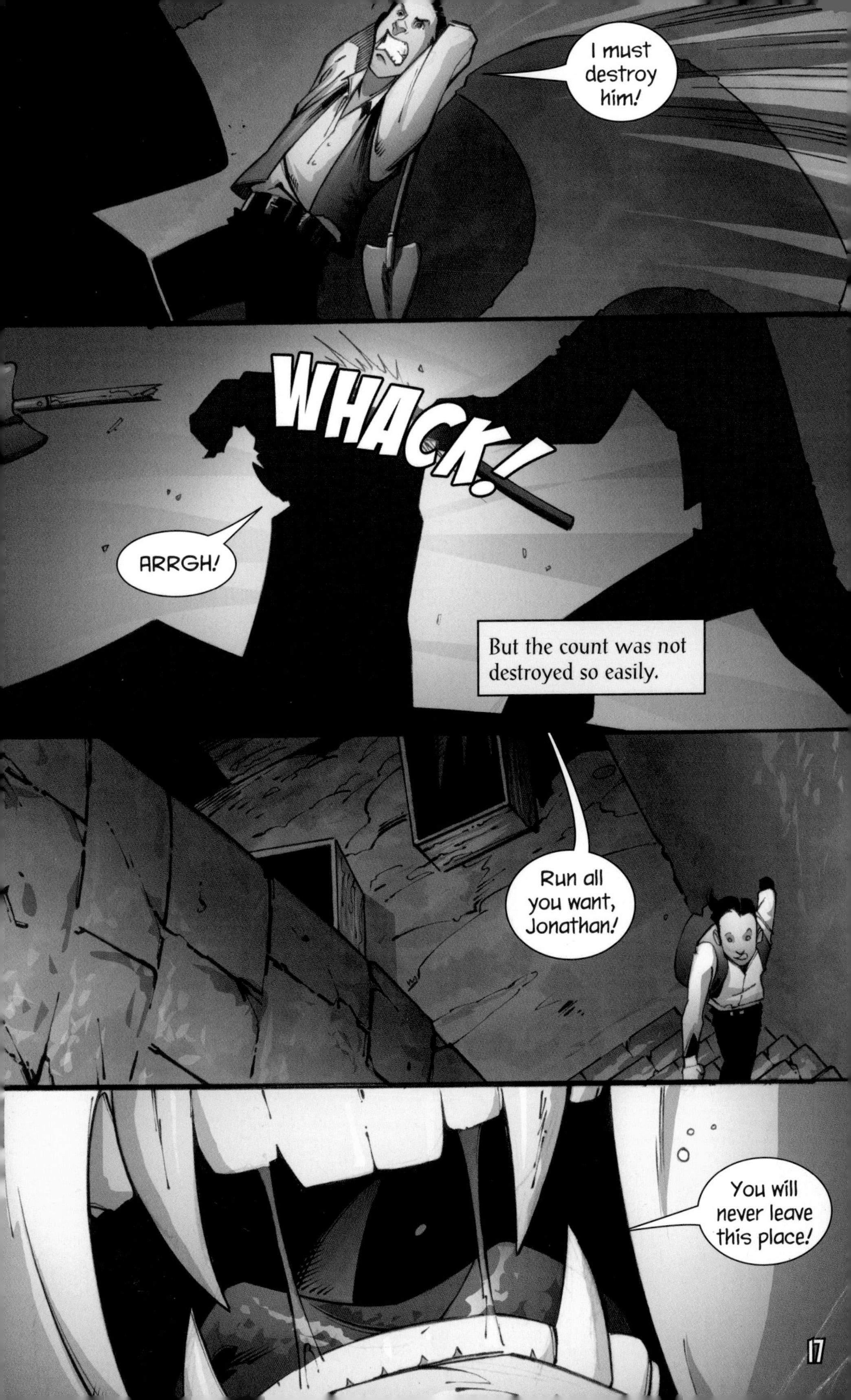
I must destroy him!
WHACK!
ARRGH!
But the count was not destroyed so easily.
Run all you want, Jonathan!
You will never leave this place!

CHAPTER 2: DANGERS IN THE NIGHT

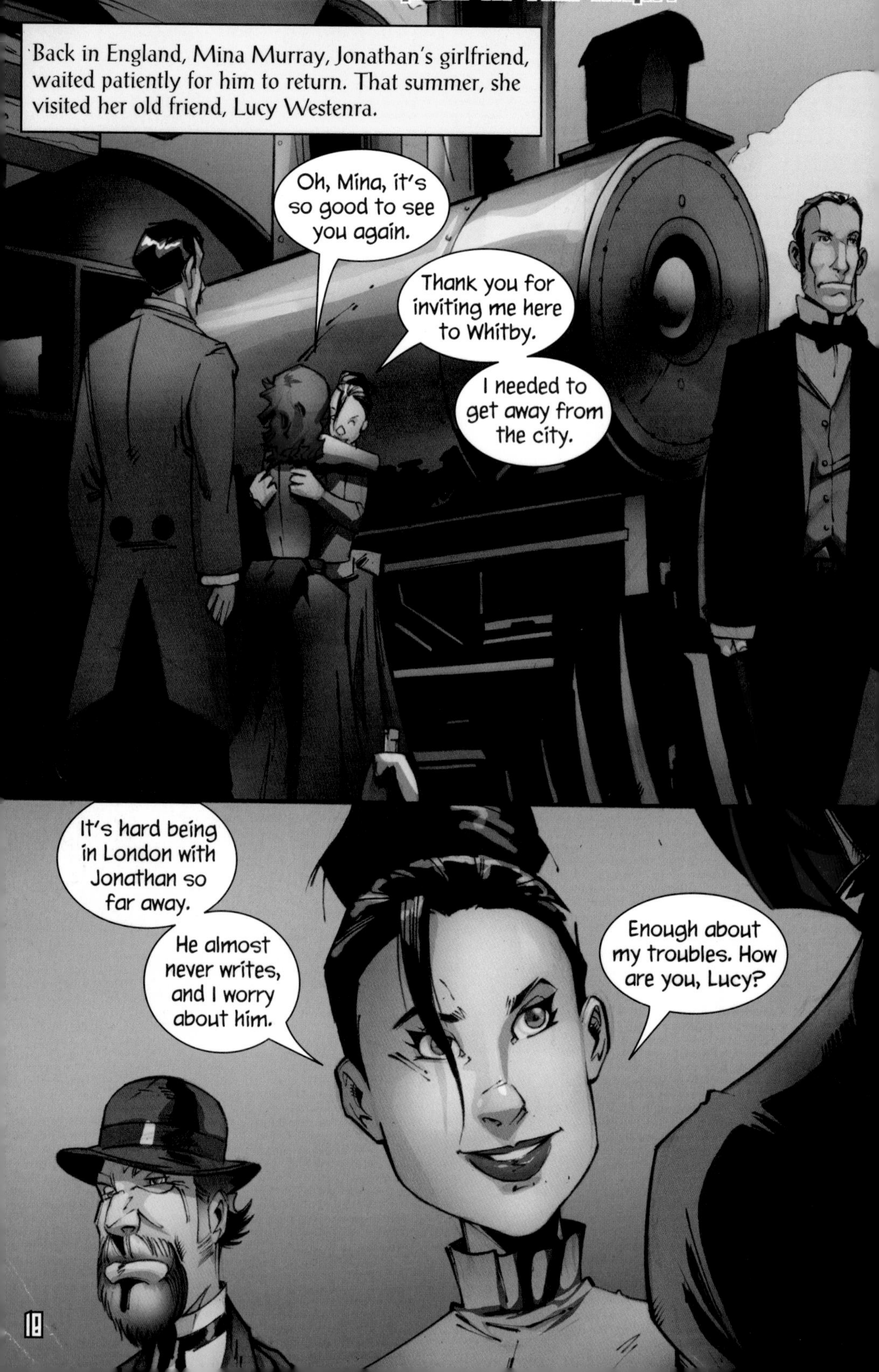
Back in England, Mina Murray, Jonathan's girlfriend, waited patiently for him to return. That summer, she visited her old friend, Lucy Westenra.
Oh, Mina, it's so good to see you again.
Thank you for inviting me here to Whitby.
I needed to get away from the city.
It's hard being in London with Jonathan so far away.
He almost never writes, and I worry about him.
Enough about my troubles. How are you, Lucy?

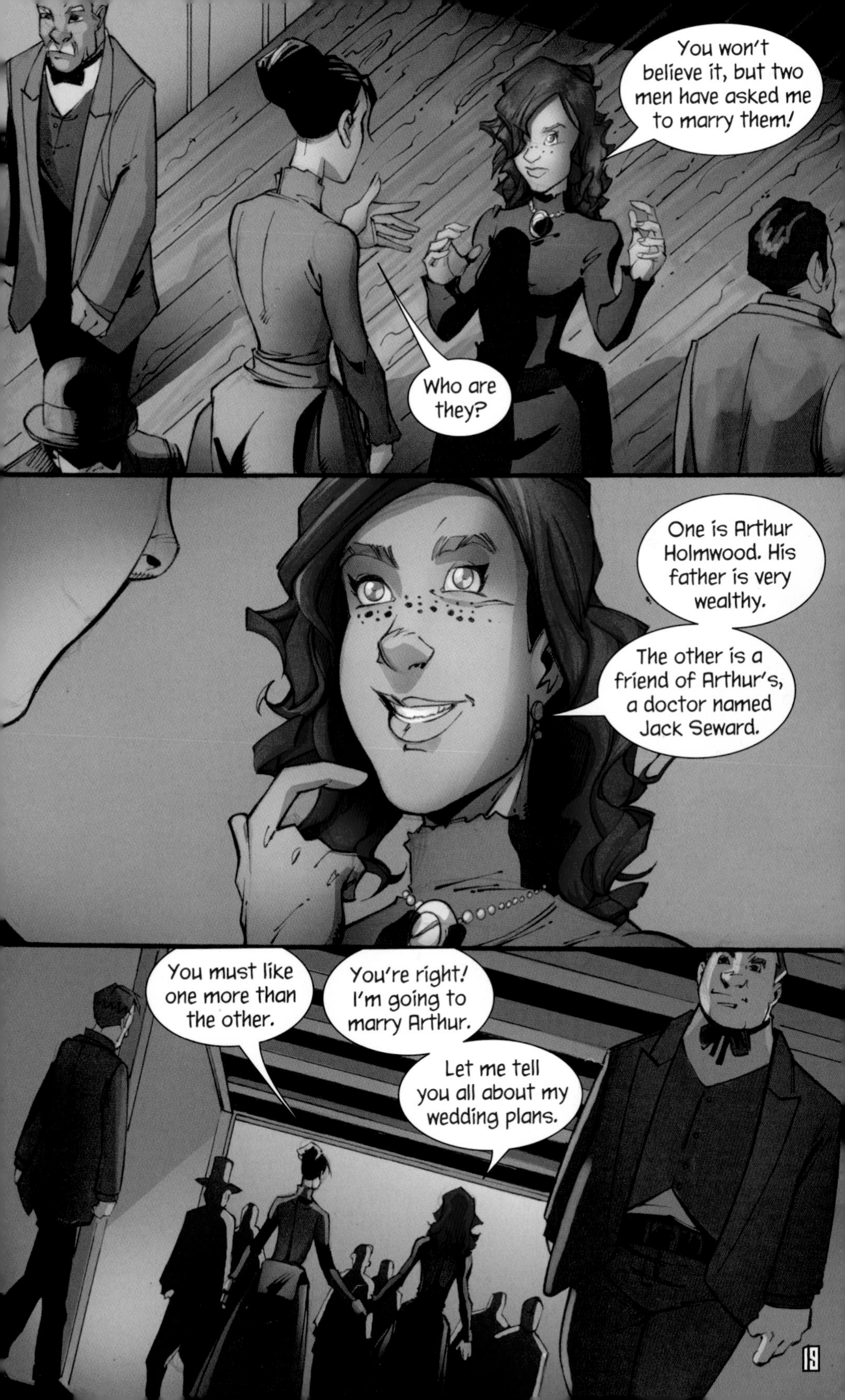
You won't believe it, but two men have asked me to marry them!
Who are they?
One is Arthur Holmwood. His father is very wealthy.
The other is a friend of Arthur's, a doctor named Jack Seward.
You must like one more than the other.
You're right! I'm going to marry Arthur.
Let me tell you all about my wedding plans.

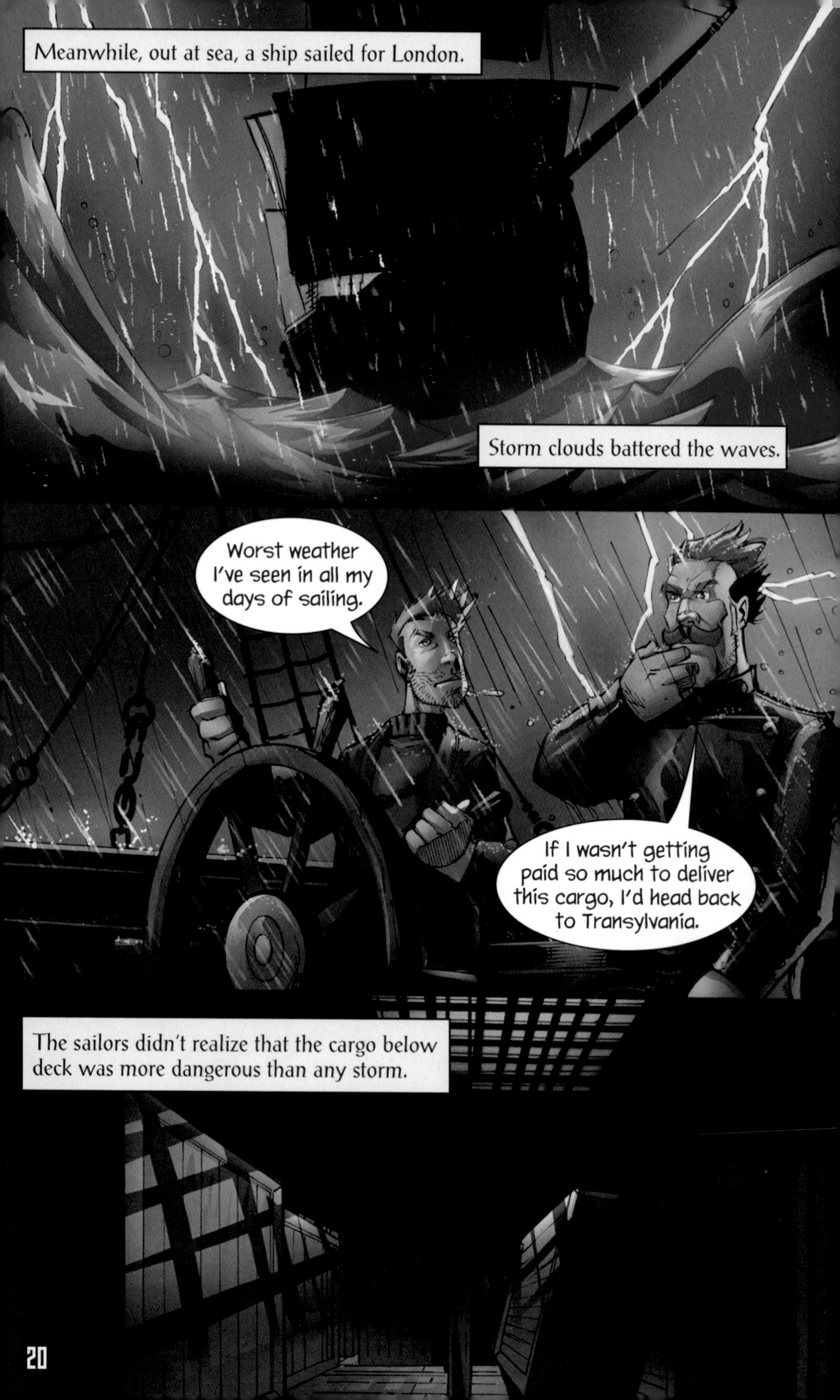
Meanwhile, out at sea, a ship sailed for London.
Storm clouds battered the waves.
Worst weather I've seen in all my days of sailing.
If I wasn't getting paid so much to deliver this cargo, I'd head back to Transylvania.
The sailors didn't realize that the cargo below deck was more dangerous than any storm.

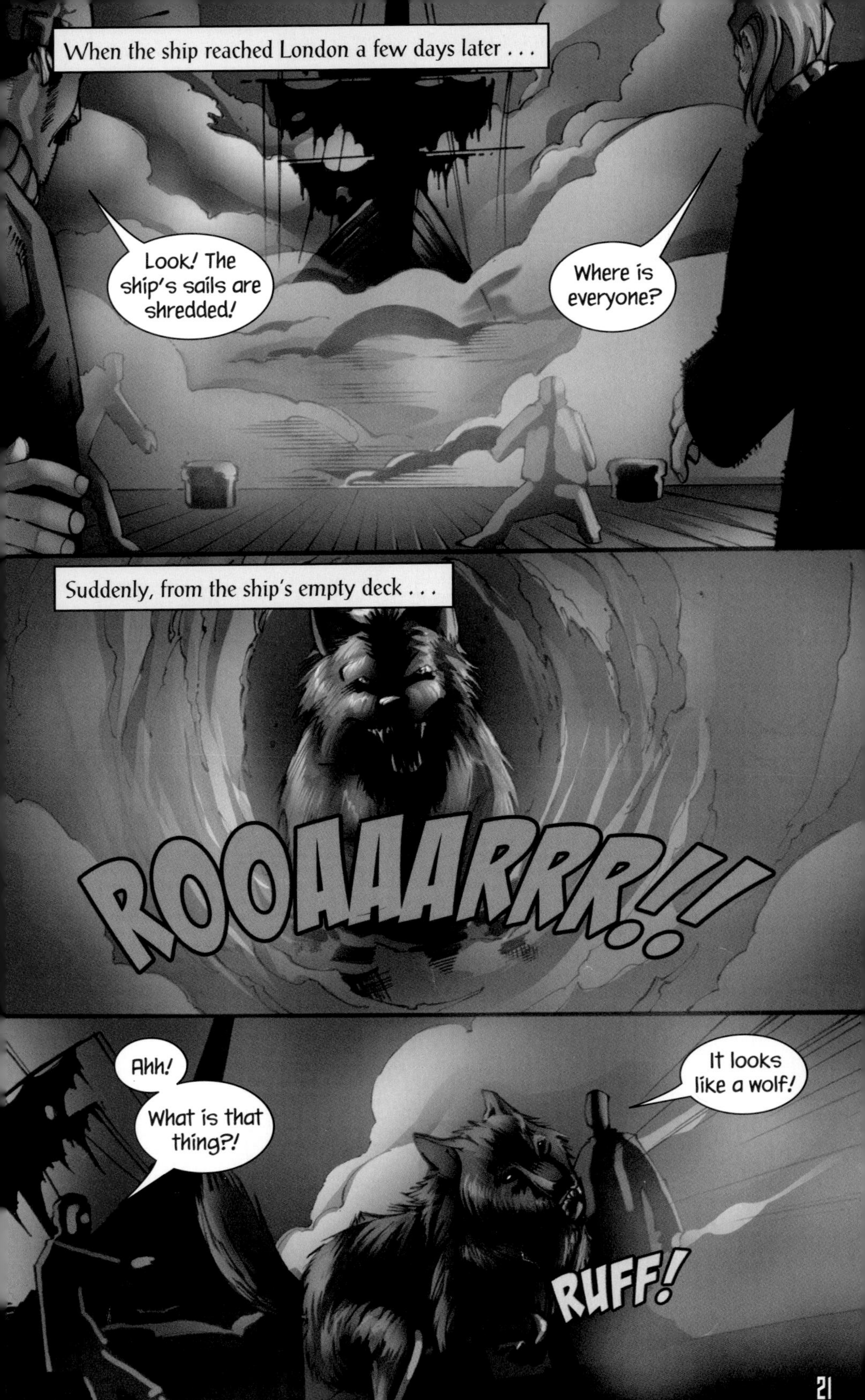
When the ship reached London a few days later . . .
Look! The ship's sails are shredded!
Where is everyone?
Suddenly, from the ship's empty deck . . .
ROOAAARRR!!
Ahh!
What is that thing?!
It looks like a wolf!
RUFF!

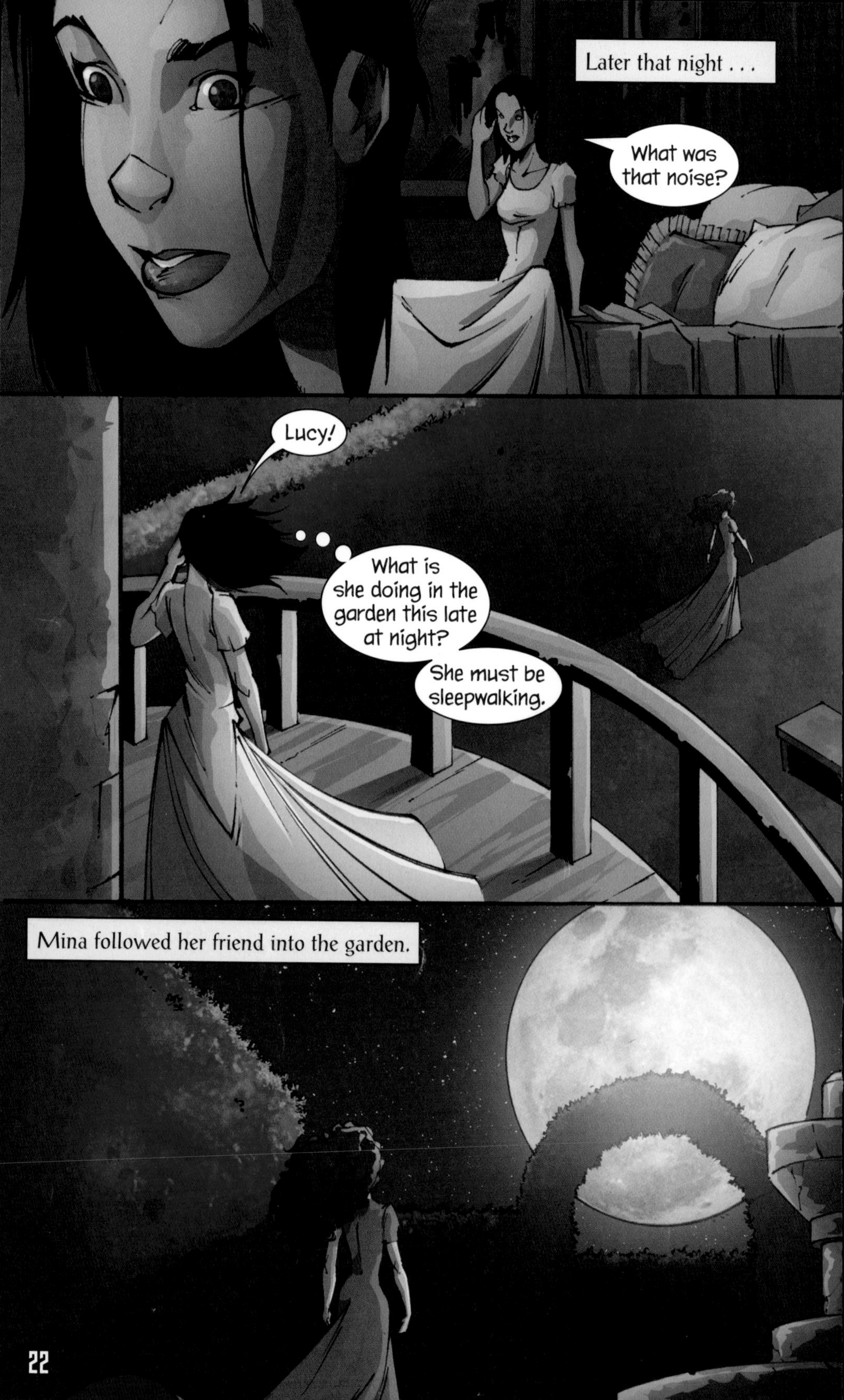
Later that night . . .
What was that noise?
Lucy!
What is she doing in the garden this late at night?
She must be sleepwalking.
Mina followed her friend into the garden.

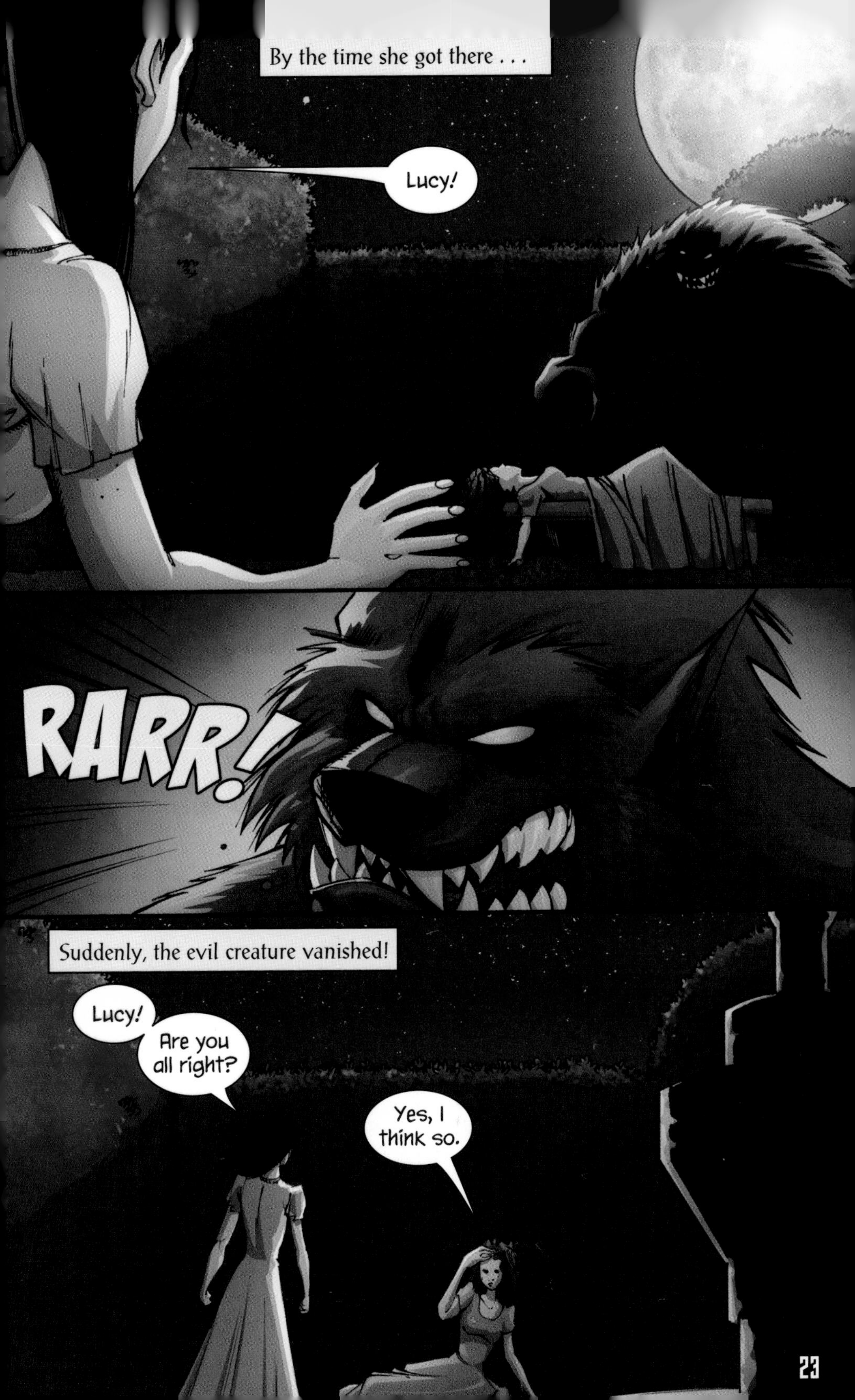

By the time she got there . . .
Lucy!
RARR!
Suddenly, the evil creature vanished!
Lucy!
Are you all right?
Yes, I think so.

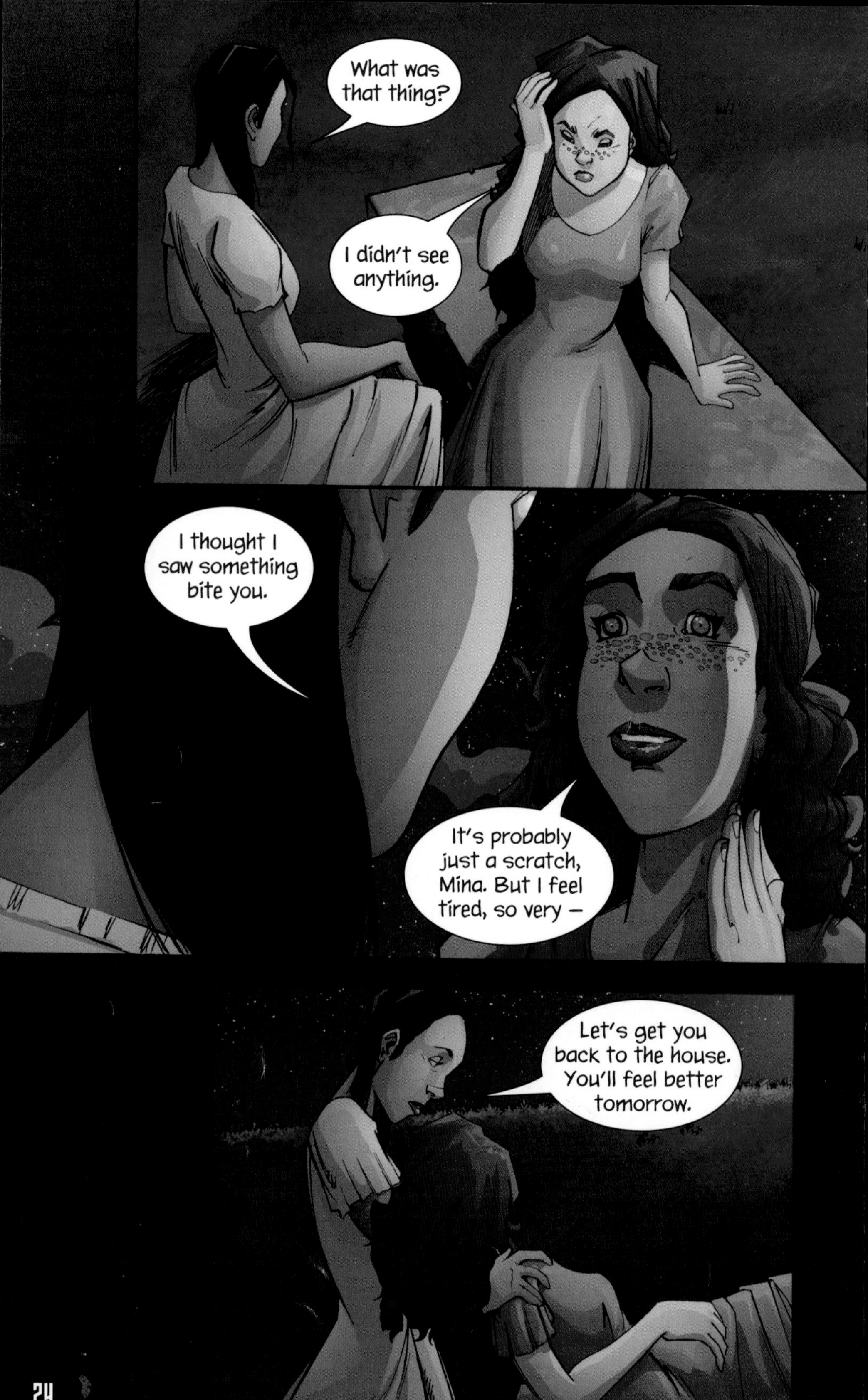
What was that thing?
I didn't see anything.
I thought I saw something bite you.
It's probably just a scratch, Mina. But I feel tired, so very —
Let's get you back to the house. You'll feel better tomorrow.

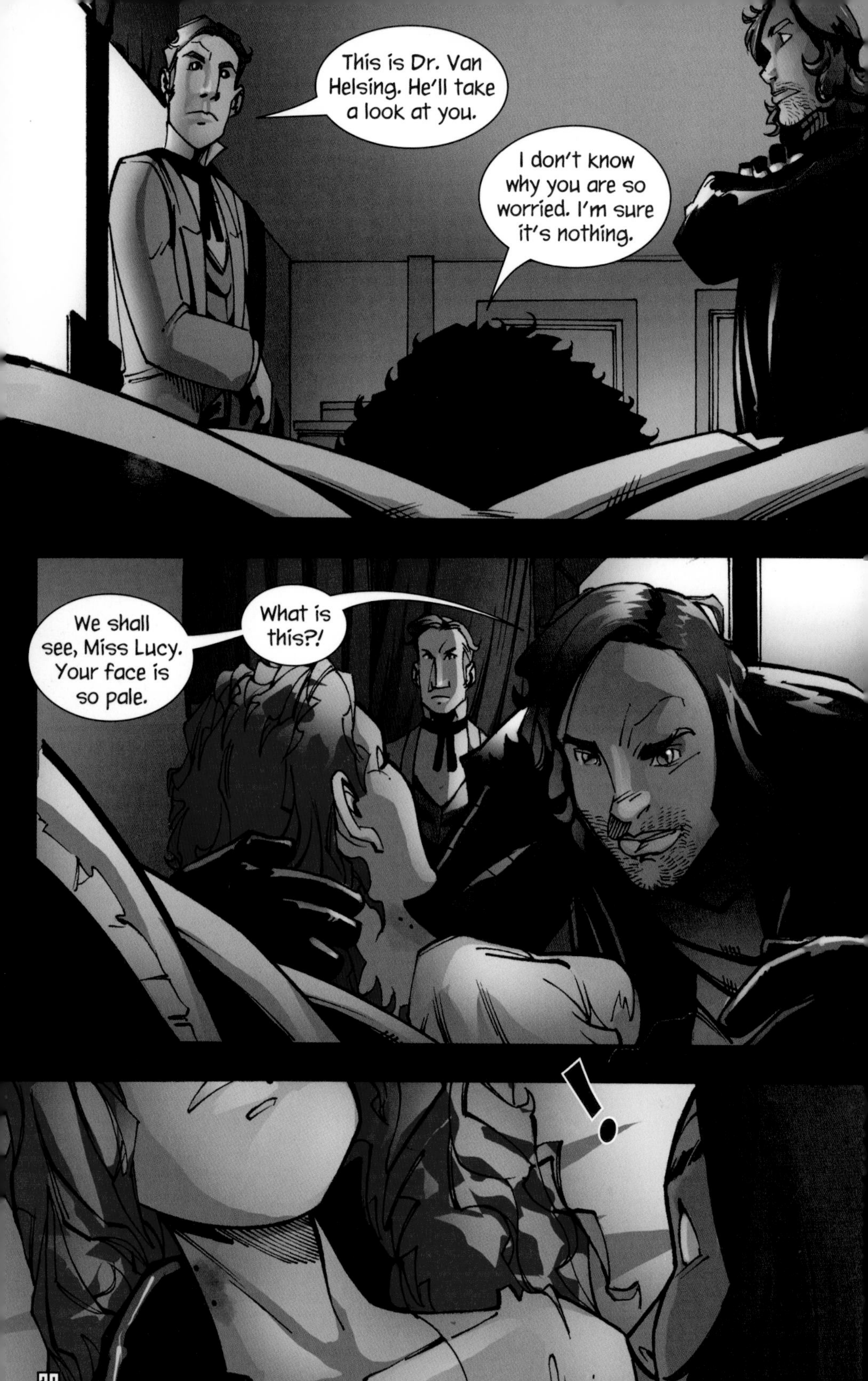
This is Dr. Van Helsing. He'll take a look at you.
I don't know why you are so worried. I'm sure it's nothing.
We shall see, Miss Lucy. Your face is so pale.
What is this?!
!

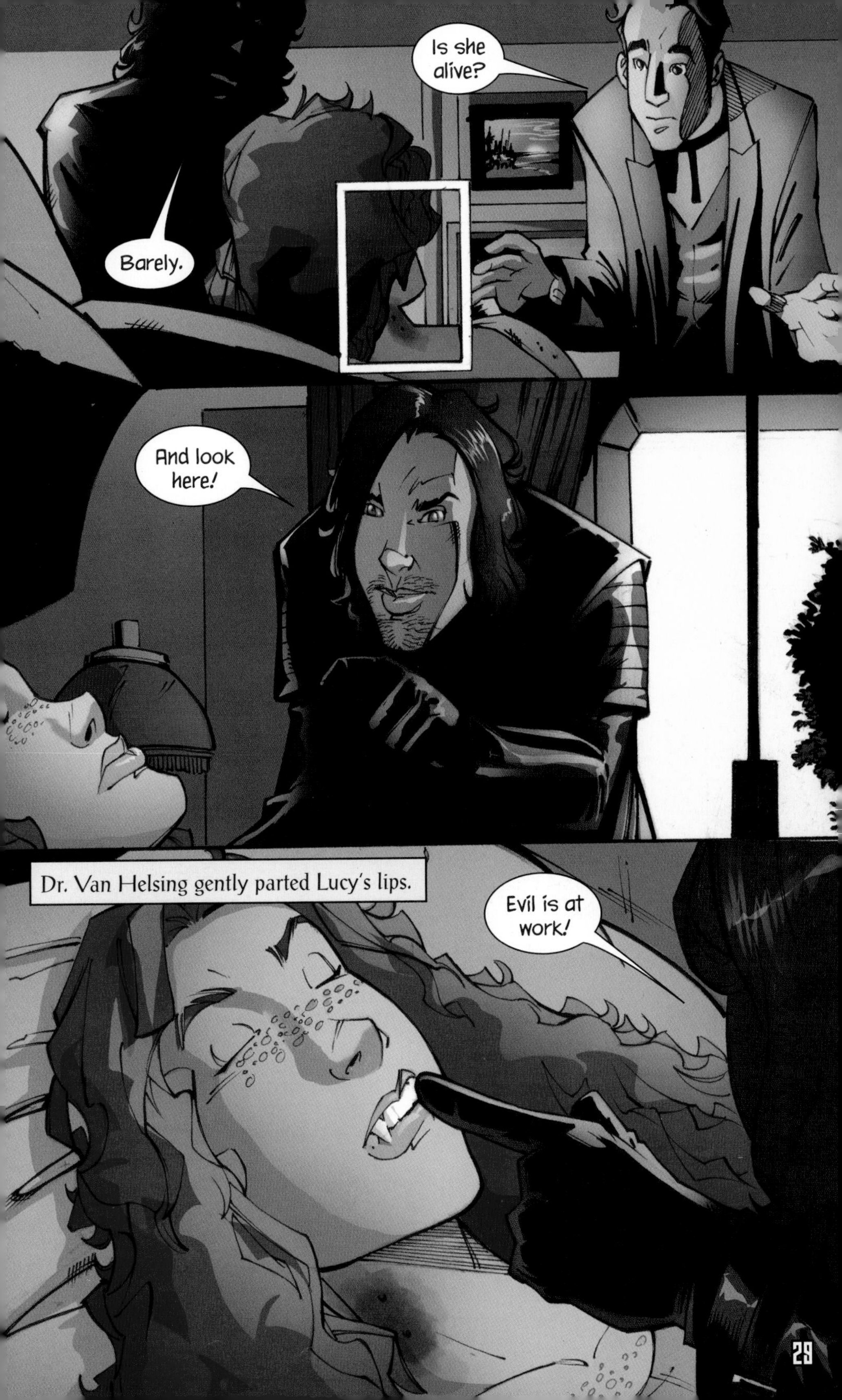
Is she alive?
Barely.
And look here!
Dr. Van Helsing gently parted Lucy's lips.
Evil is at work!

CHAPTER 3: A MYSTERIOUS DEATH

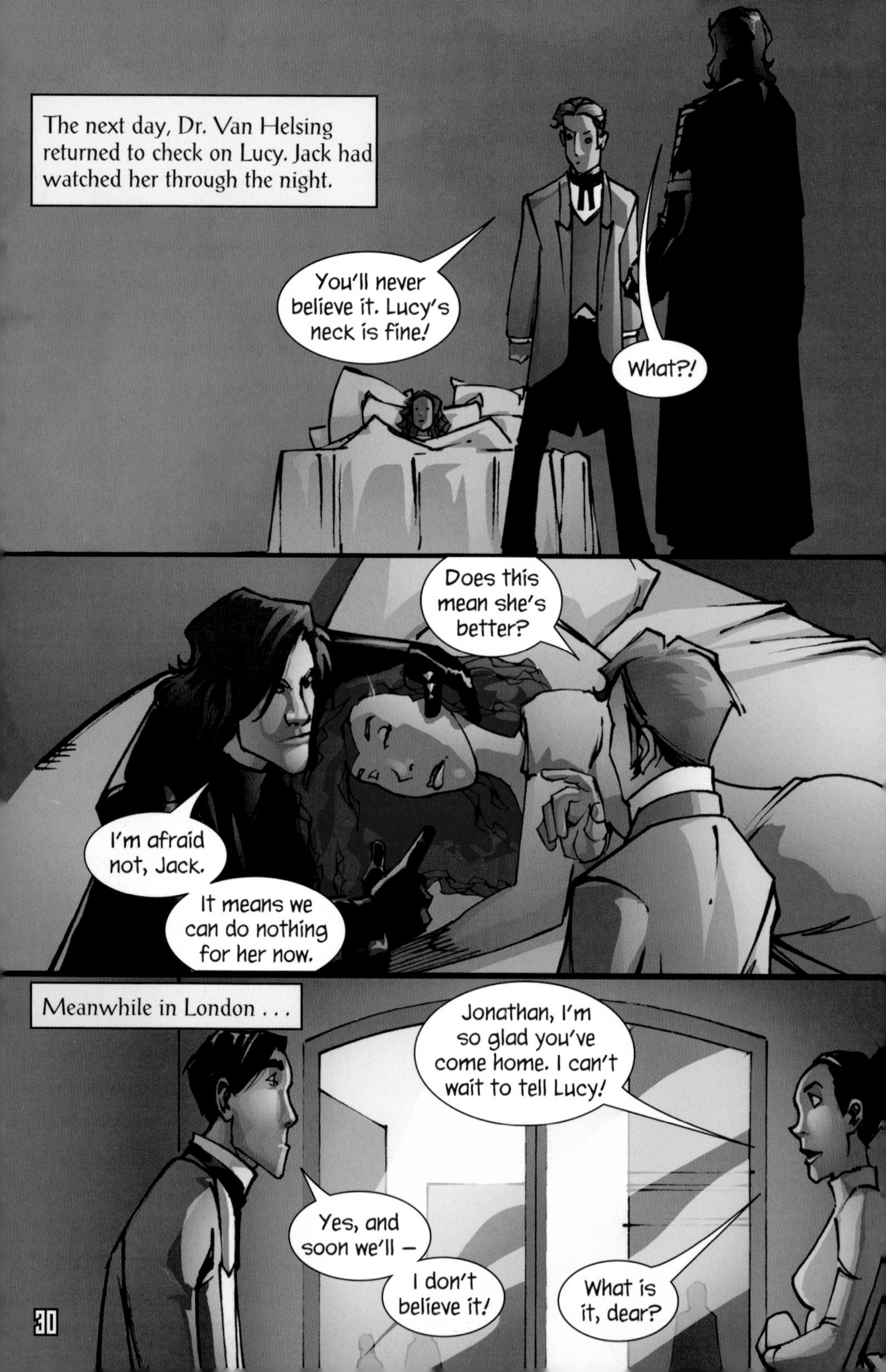
The next day, Dr. Van Helsing returned to check on Lucy. Jack had watched her through the night.
You'll never believe it. Lucy's neck is fine!
What?!
Does this mean she's better?
I'm afraid not, Jack.
It means we can do nothing for her now.
Meanwhile in London . . .
Jonathan, I'm so glad you've come home. I can't wait to tell Lucy!
Yes, and soon we'll —
I don't believe it!
What is it, dear?

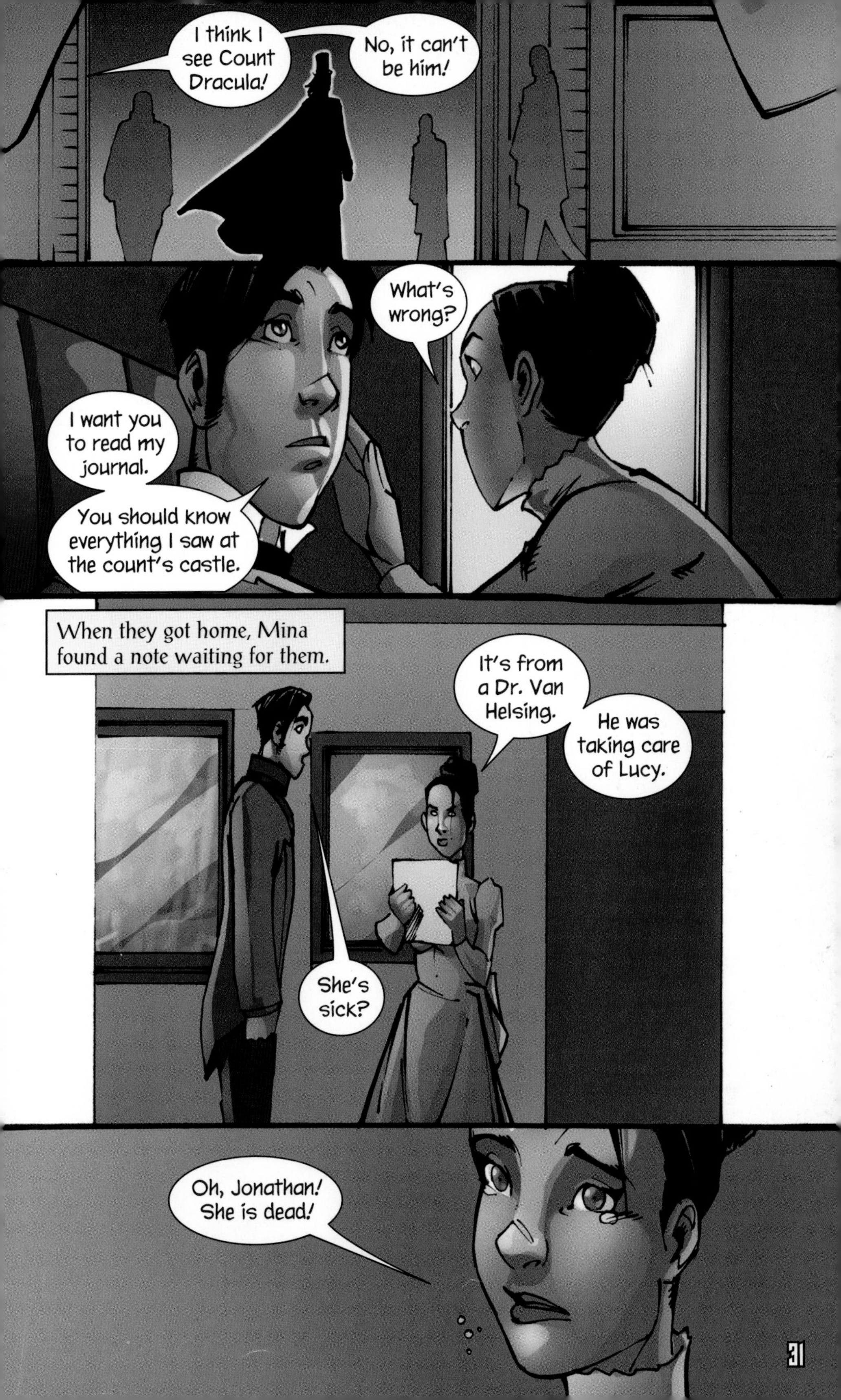
I think I see Count Dracula!
No, it can't be him!
What's wrong?
I want you to read my journal.
You should know everything I saw at the count's castle.
When they got home, Mina found a note waiting for them.
It's from a Dr. Van Helsing.
He was taking care of Lucy.
She's sick?
Oh, Jonathan! She is dead!

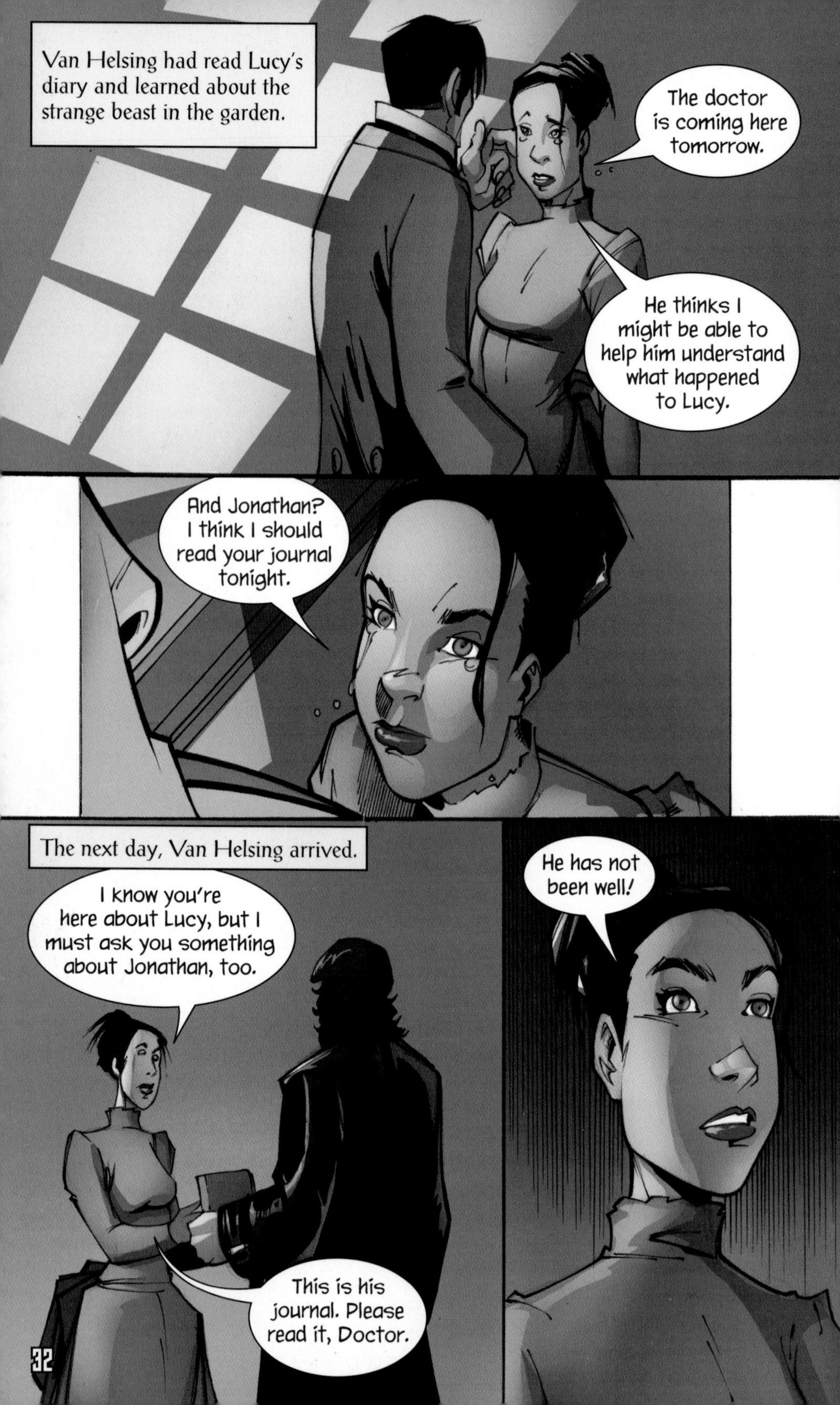
Van Helsing had read Lucy's diary and learned about the strange beast in the garden.
The doctor is coming here tomorrow.
He thinks I might be able to help him understand what happened to Lucy.
And Jonathan? I think I should read your journal tonight.
The next day, Van Helsing arrived.
I know you're here about Lucy, but I must ask you something about Jonathan, too.
This is his journal. Please read it, Doctor.
He has not been well!

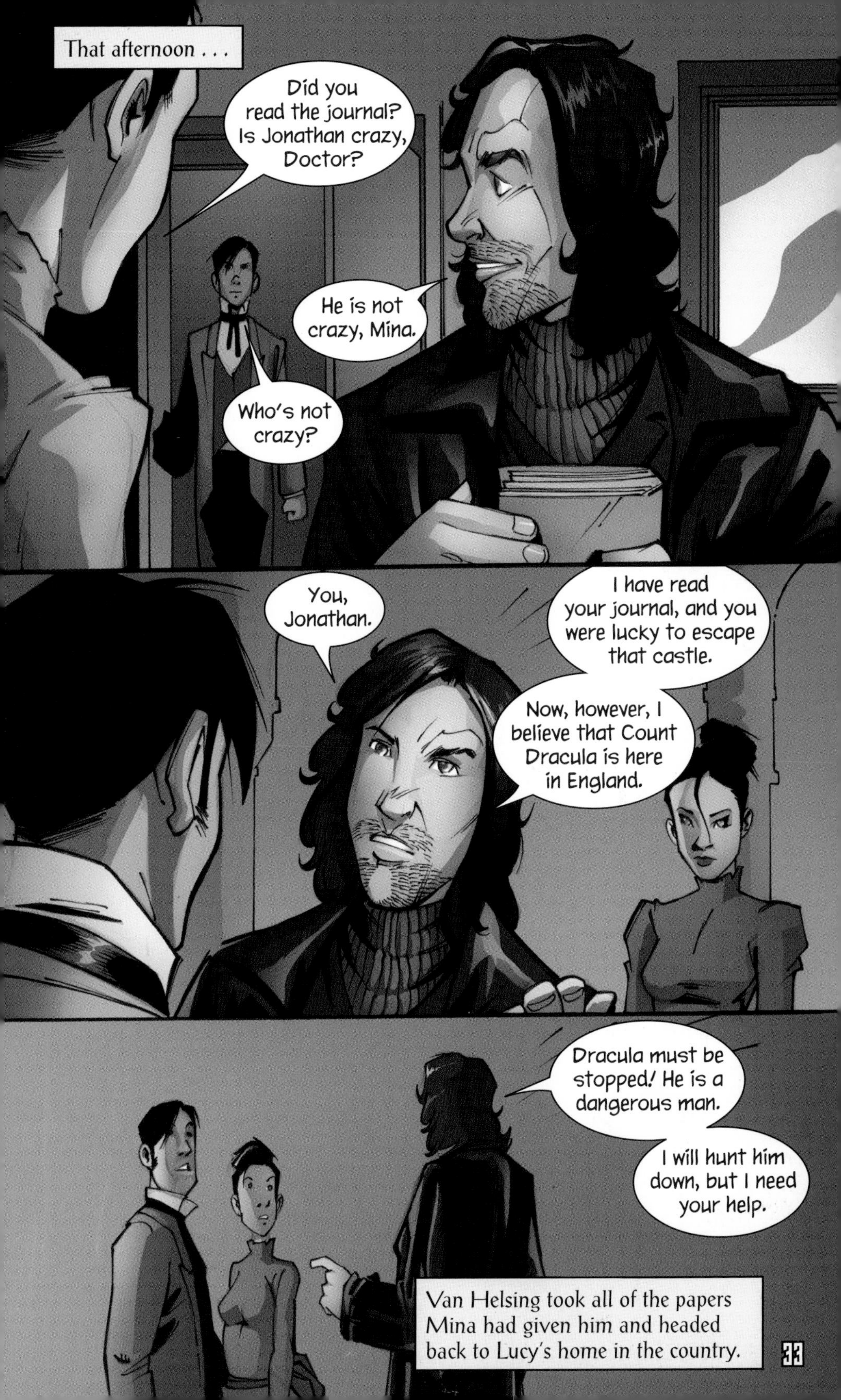
That afternoon . . .
Did you read the journal? Is Jonathan crazy, Doctor?
He is not crazy, Mina.
Who's not crazy?
You, Jonathan.
I have read your journal, and you were lucky to escape that castle.
Now, however, I believe that Count Dracula is here in England.
Dracula must be stopped! He is a dangerous man.
I will hunt him down, but I need your help.
Van Helsing took all of the papers Mina had given him and headed back to Lucy's home in the country.

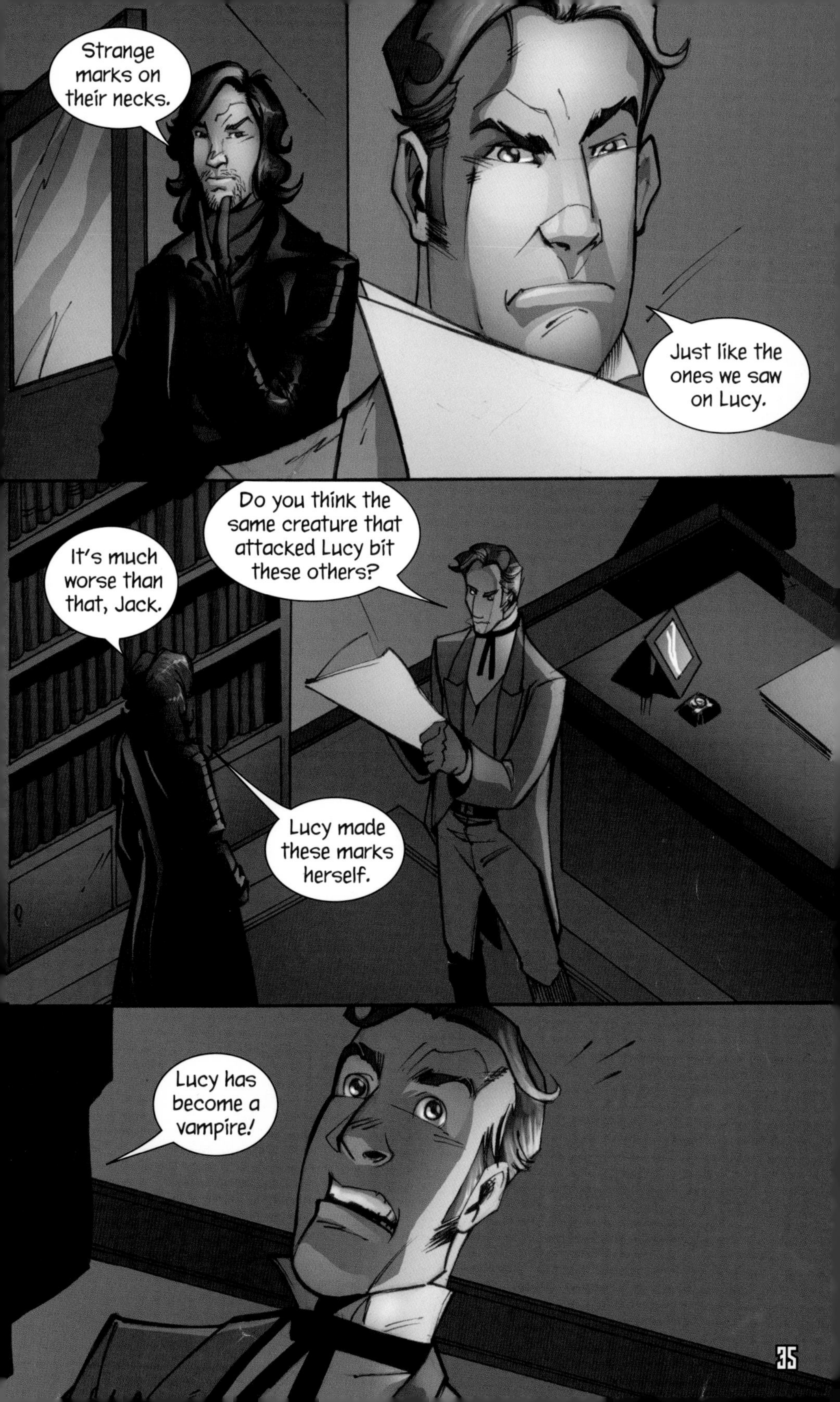
Strange marks on their necks.
Just like the ones we saw on Lucy.
Do you think the same creature that attacked Lucy bit these others?
It's much worse than that, Jack.
Lucy made these marks herself.
Lucy has become a vampire!

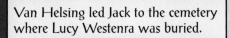

Van Helsing led Jack to the cemetery where Lucy Westenra was buried.

WESTENRA

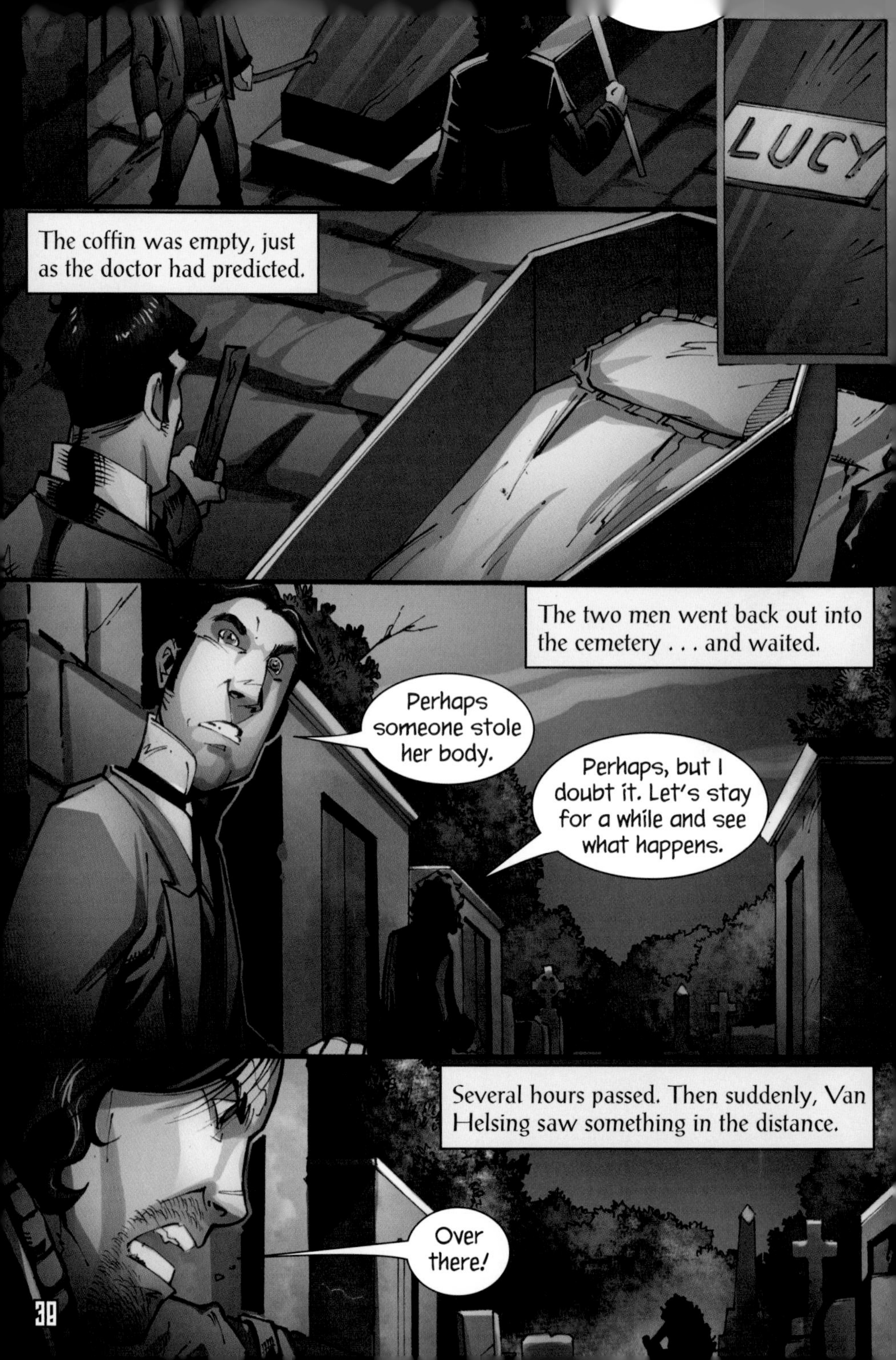
LUCY
The coffin was empty, just as the doctor had predicted.
The two men went back out into the cemetery . . . and waited.
Perhaps someone stole her body.
Perhaps, but I doubt it. Let's stay for a while and see what happens.
Several hours passed. Then suddenly, Van Helsing saw something in the distance.
Over there!

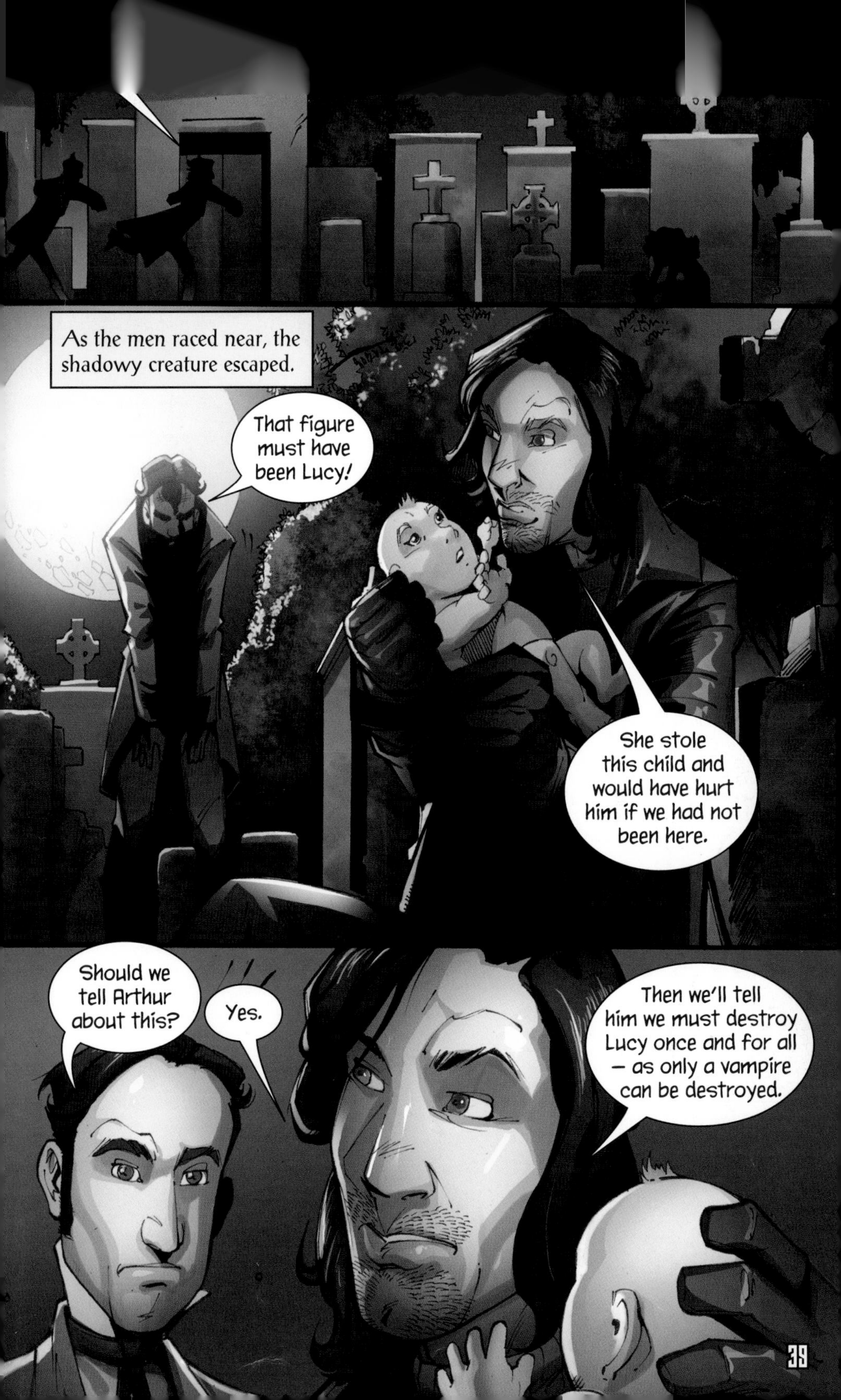
As the men raced near, the shadowy creature escaped.
That figure must have been Lucy!
She stole this child and would have hurt him if we had not been here.
Should we tell Arthur about this?
Yes.
Then we'll tell him we must destroy Lucy once and for all — as only a vampire can be destroyed.

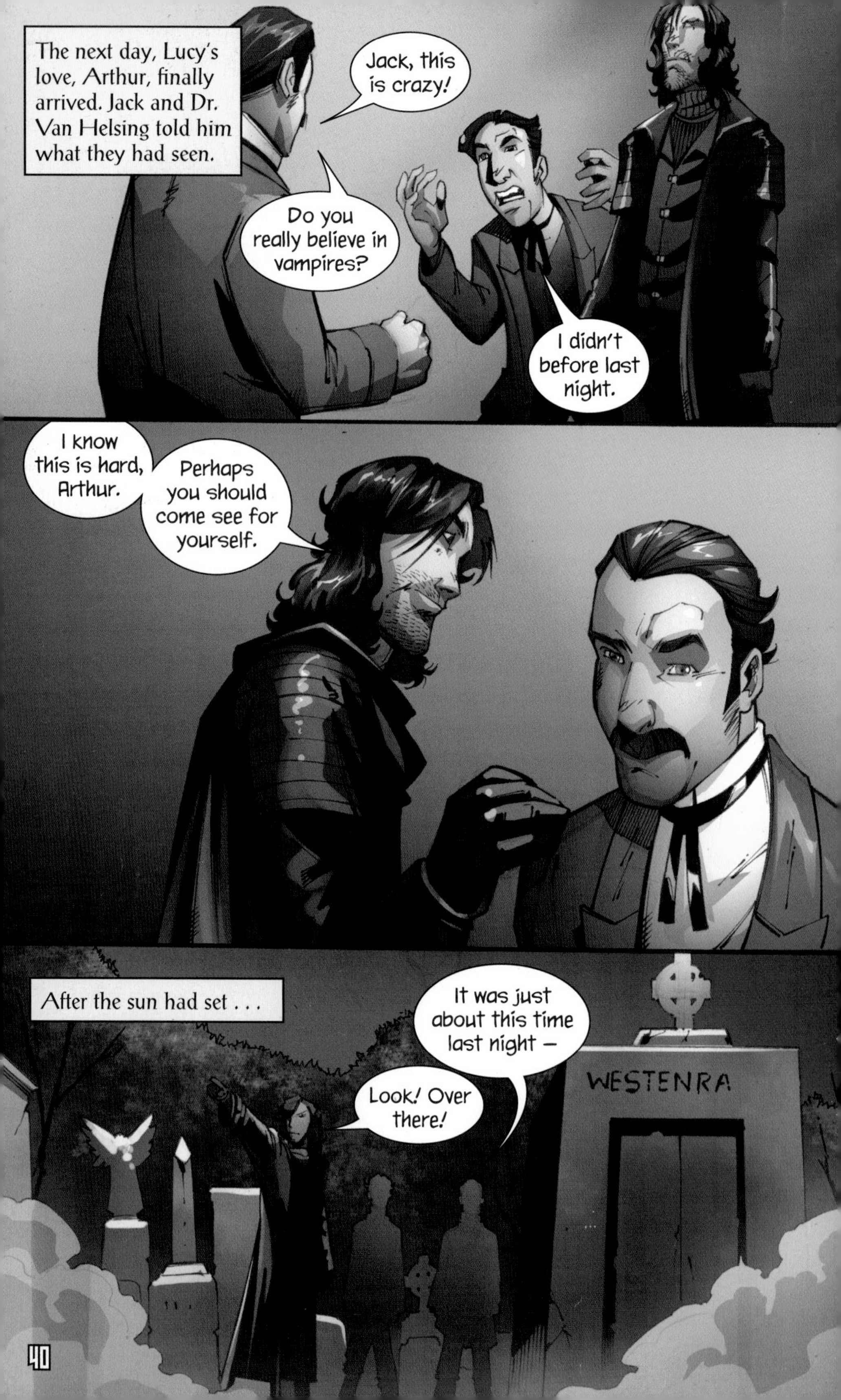

The next day, Lucy's love, Arthur, finally arrived. Jack and Dr. Van Helsing told him what they had seen.
Jack, this is crazy!
Do you really believe in vampires?
I didn't before last night.
I know this is hard, Arthur.
Perhaps you should come see for yourself.
After the sun had set . . .
It was just about this time last night –
Look! Over there!
WESTENRA

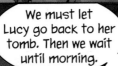

Lucy?

No! It can't be!

We must let Lucy go back to her tomb. Then we wait until morning.

She will lose her strength when the sun is up.

ESTENRA

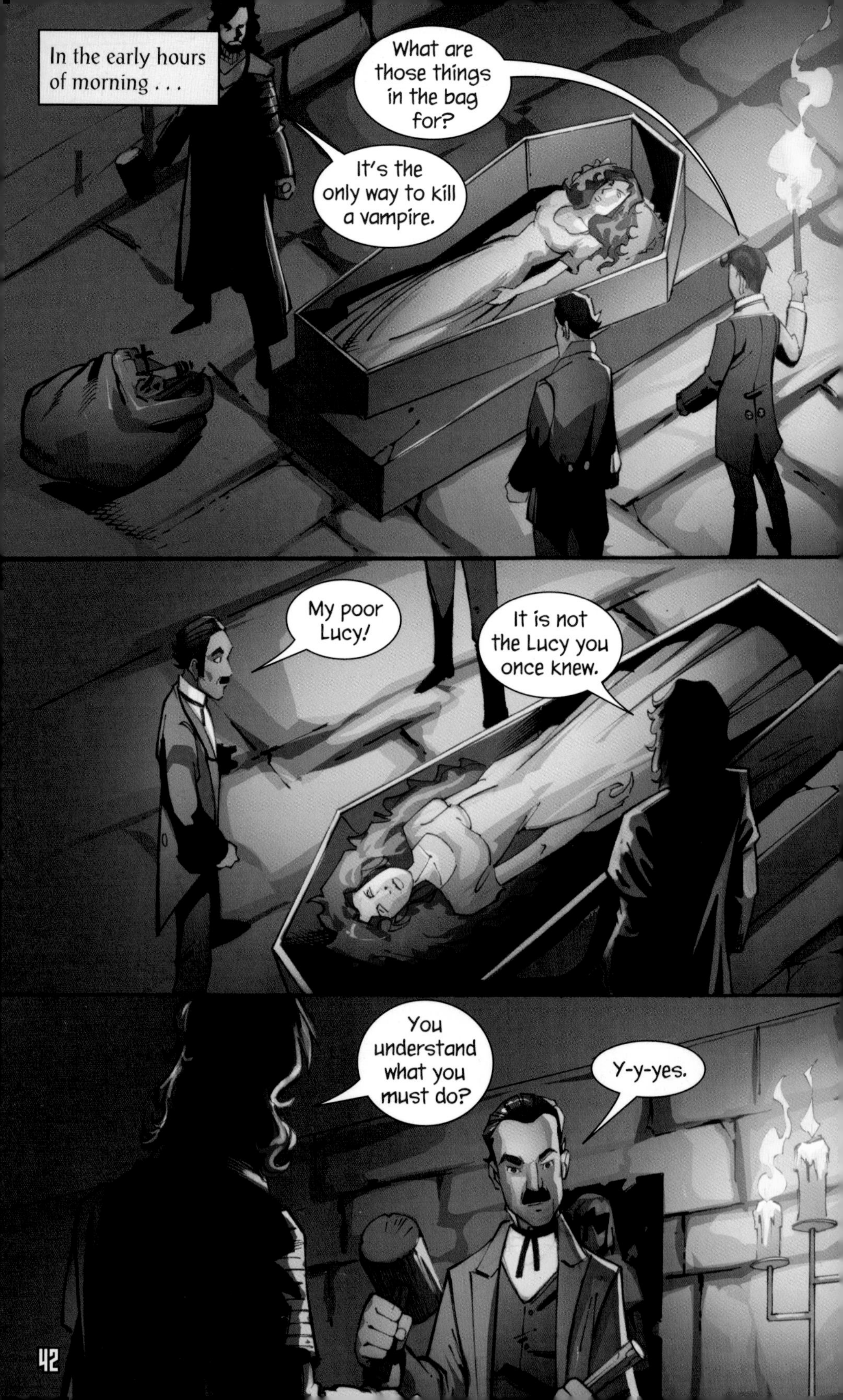

In the early hours of morning . . .
What are those things in the bag for?
It's the only way to kill a vampire.
My poor Lucy!
It is not the Lucy you once knew.
You understand what you must do?
Y-y-yes.

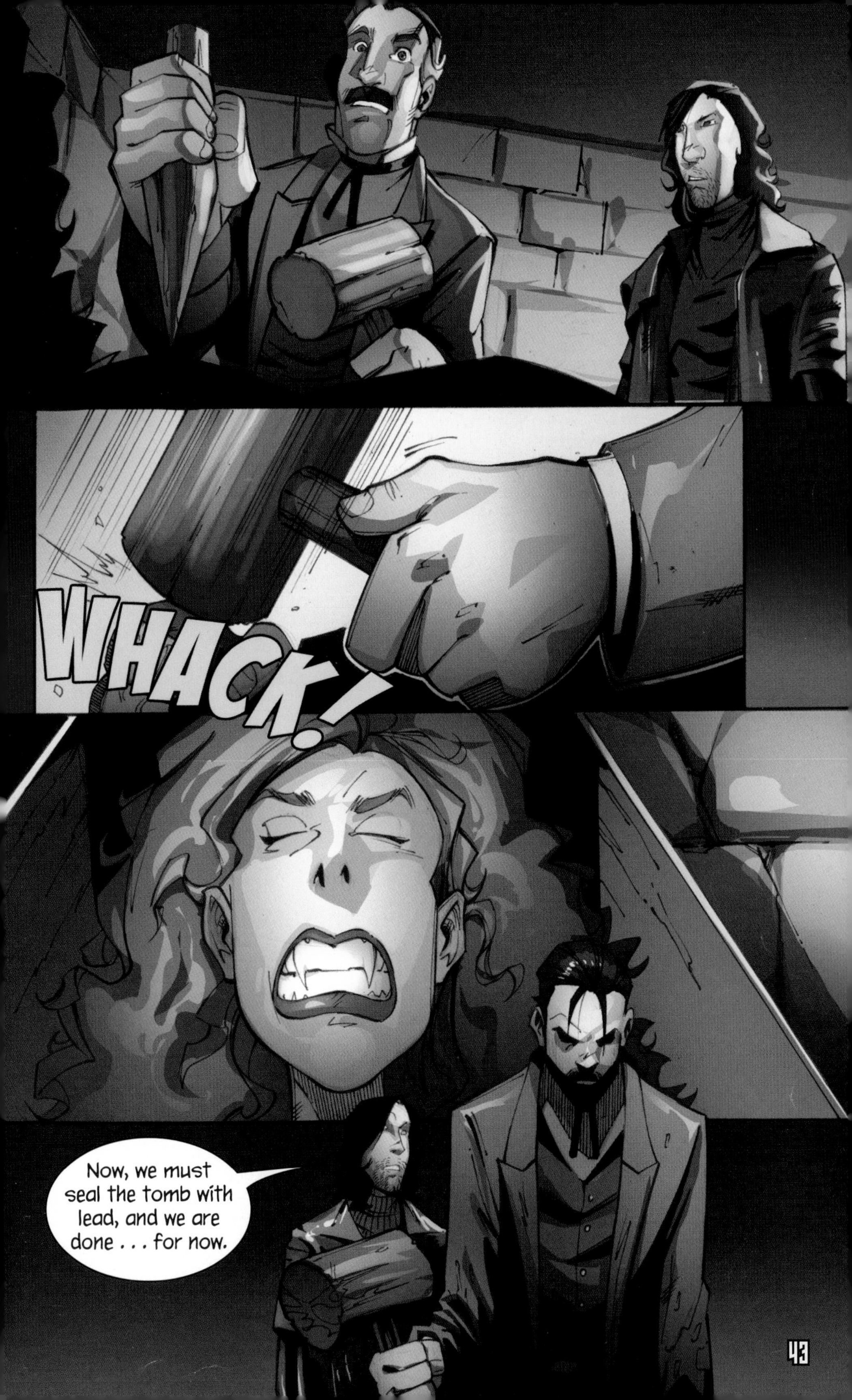
WHACK!
Now, we must seal the tomb with lead, and we are done . . . for now.

CHAPTER 5 : THE HUNT BEGINS

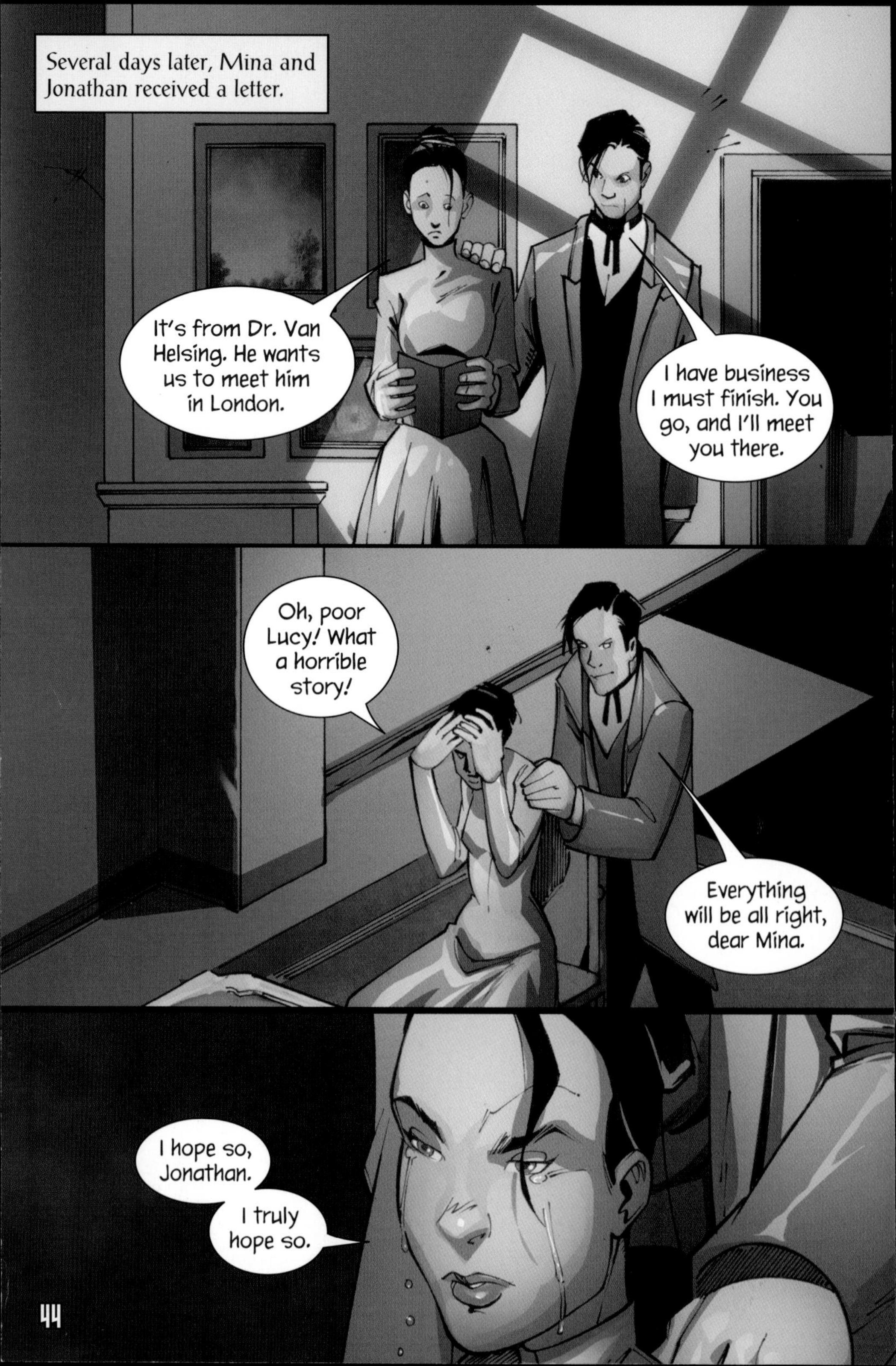
Several days later, Mina and Jonathan received a letter.
It's from Dr. Van Helsing. He wants us to meet him in London.
I have business I must finish. You go, and I'll meet you there.
Oh, poor Lucy! What a horrible story!
Everything will be all right, dear Mina.
I hope so, Jonathan.
I truly hope so.

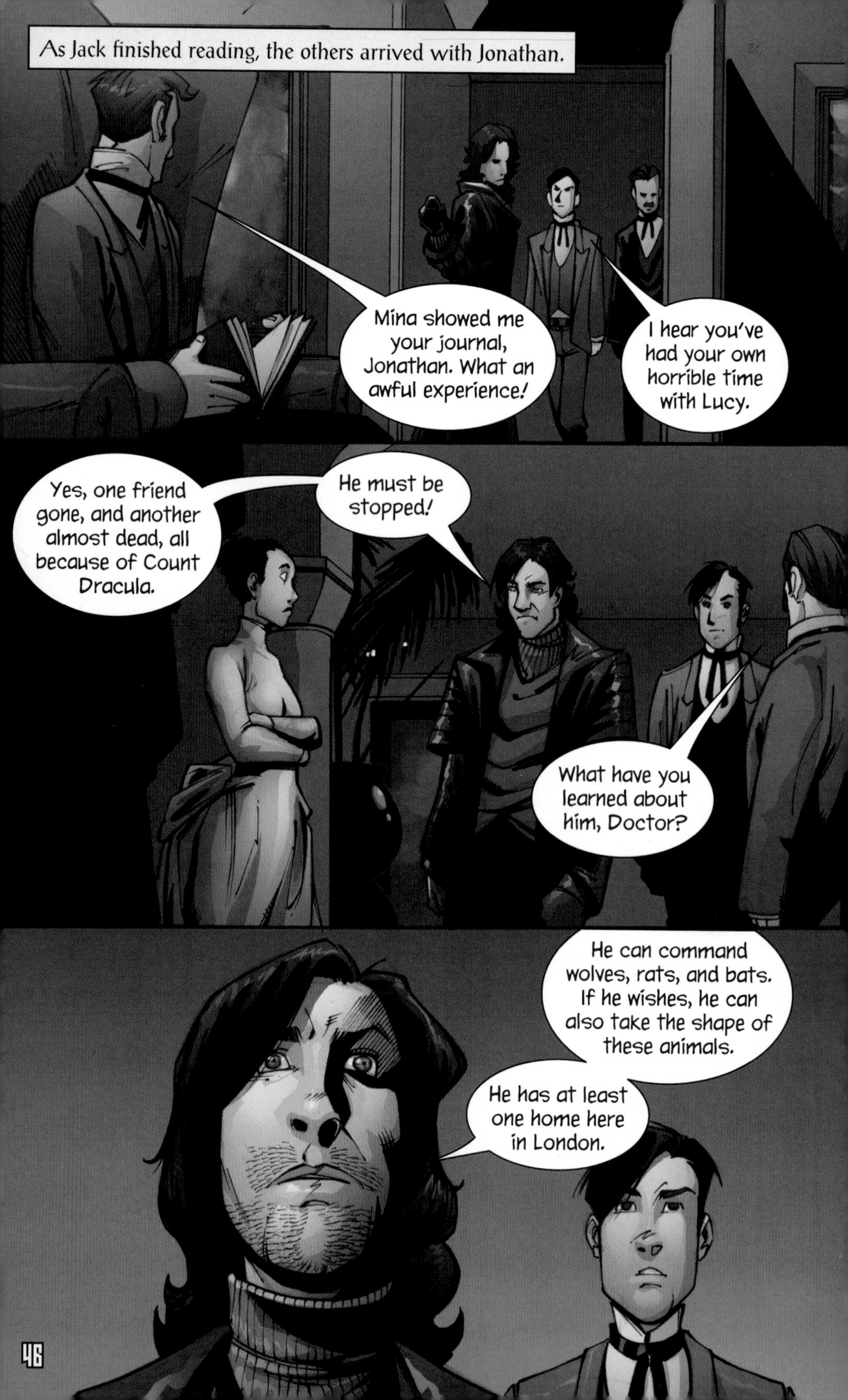
As Jack finished reading, the others arrived with Jonathan.
Mina showed me your journal, Jonathan. What an awful experience!
I hear you've had your own horrible time with Lucy.
Yes, one friend gone, and another almost dead, all because of Count Dracula.
He must be stopped!
What have you learned about him, Doctor?
He can command wolves, rats, and bats. If he wishes, he can also take the shape of these animals.
He has at least one home here in London.

I know where his new home is. It's not far from here, Doctor.
We must find the 50 boxes he shipped from Transylvania.
He can only rest in soil from his native land. Come along, gentlemen!
They soon arrived at Dracula's nearby house.
My friends, we face a terrible danger.
Before we enter this house, I have some items that will protect us.
A bottle of holy water.
A crucifix, like the one that saved Jonathan.
And a few sacred wafers. Keep them all close.

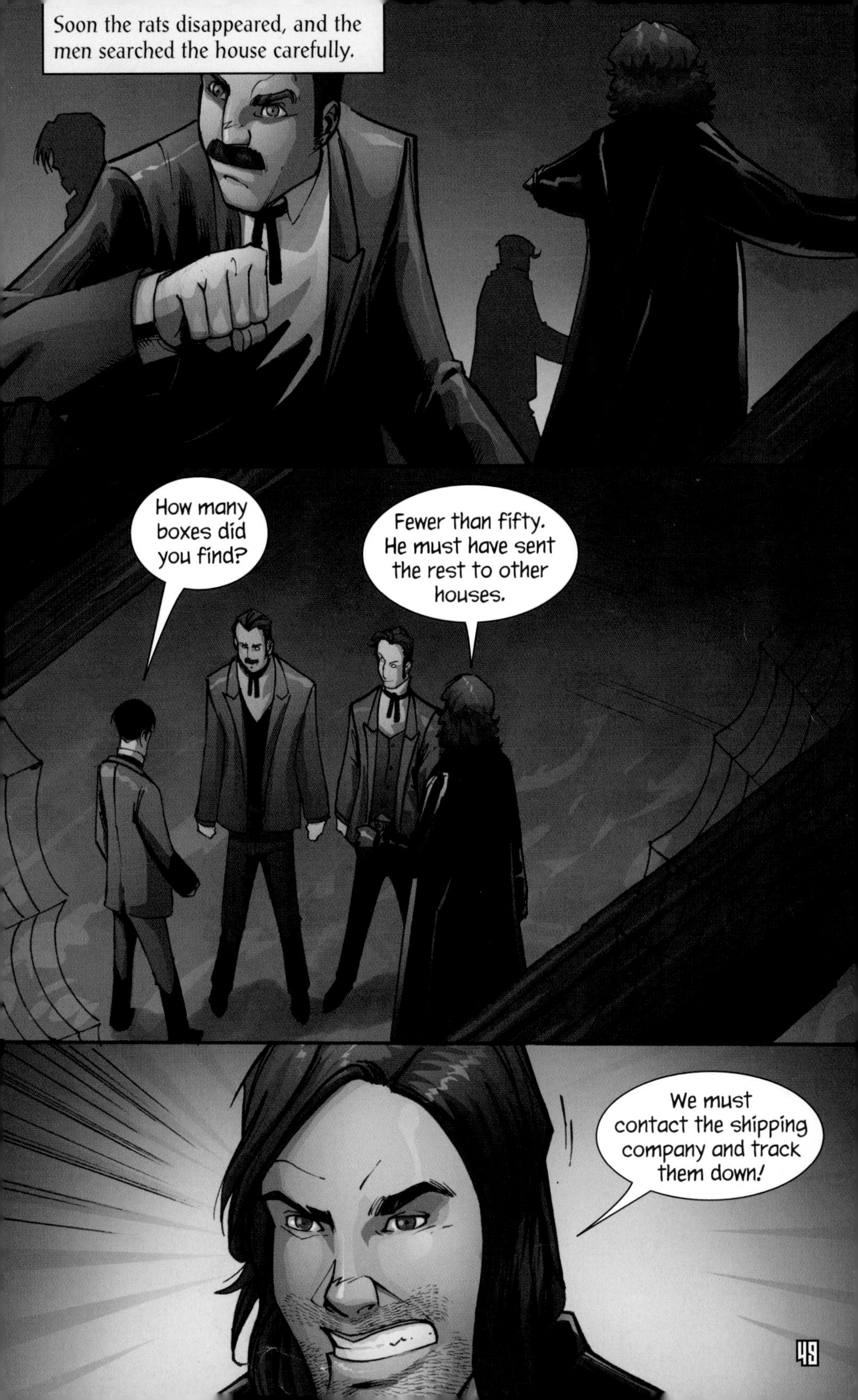
Soon the rats disappeared, and the men searched the house carefully.
How many boxes did you find?
Fewer than fifty. He must have sent the rest to other houses.
We must contact the shipping company and track them down!

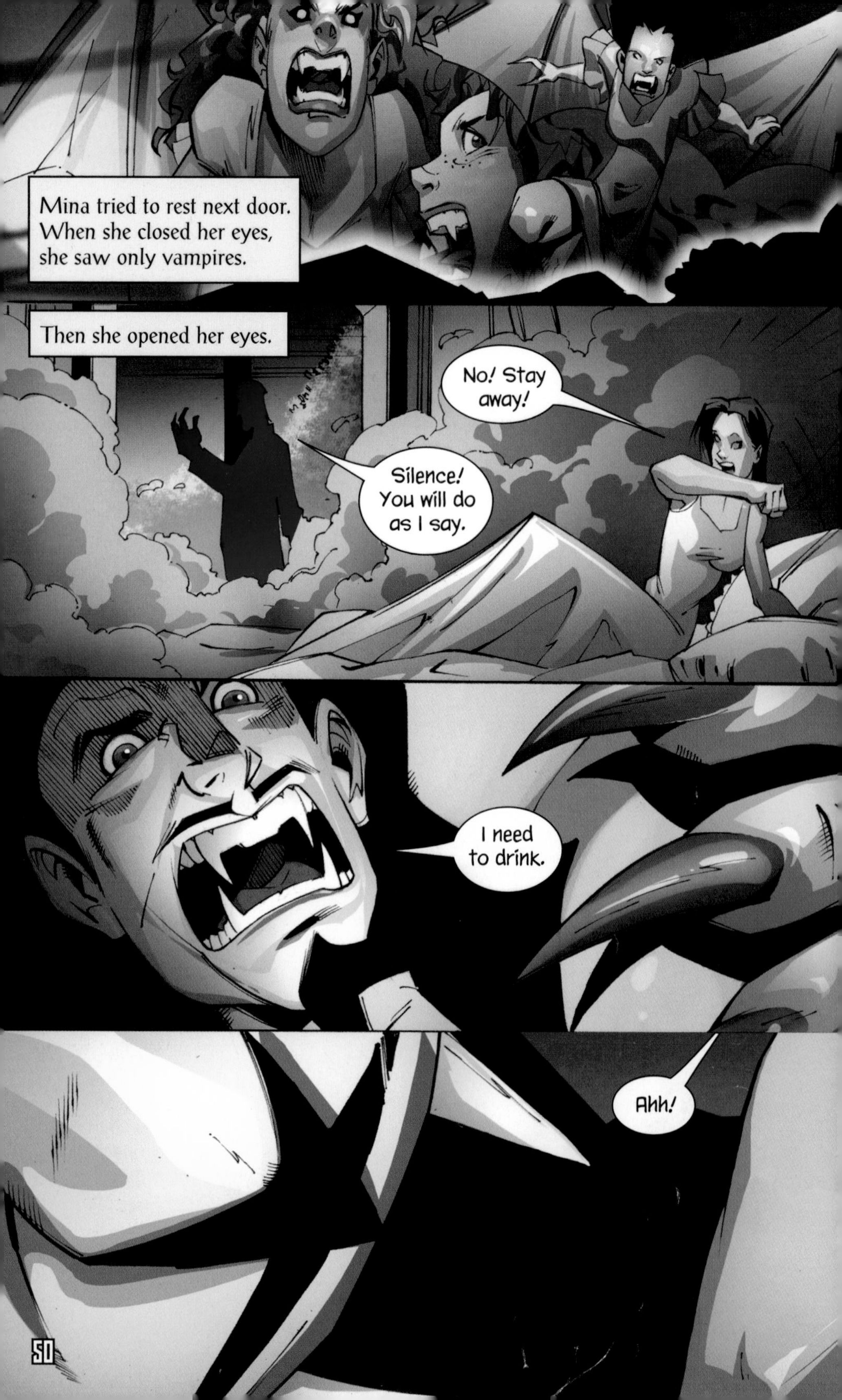
Mina tried to rest next door. When she closed her eyes, she saw only vampires.
Then she opened her eyes.
No! Stay away!
Silence! You will do as I say.
I need to drink.
Ahh!

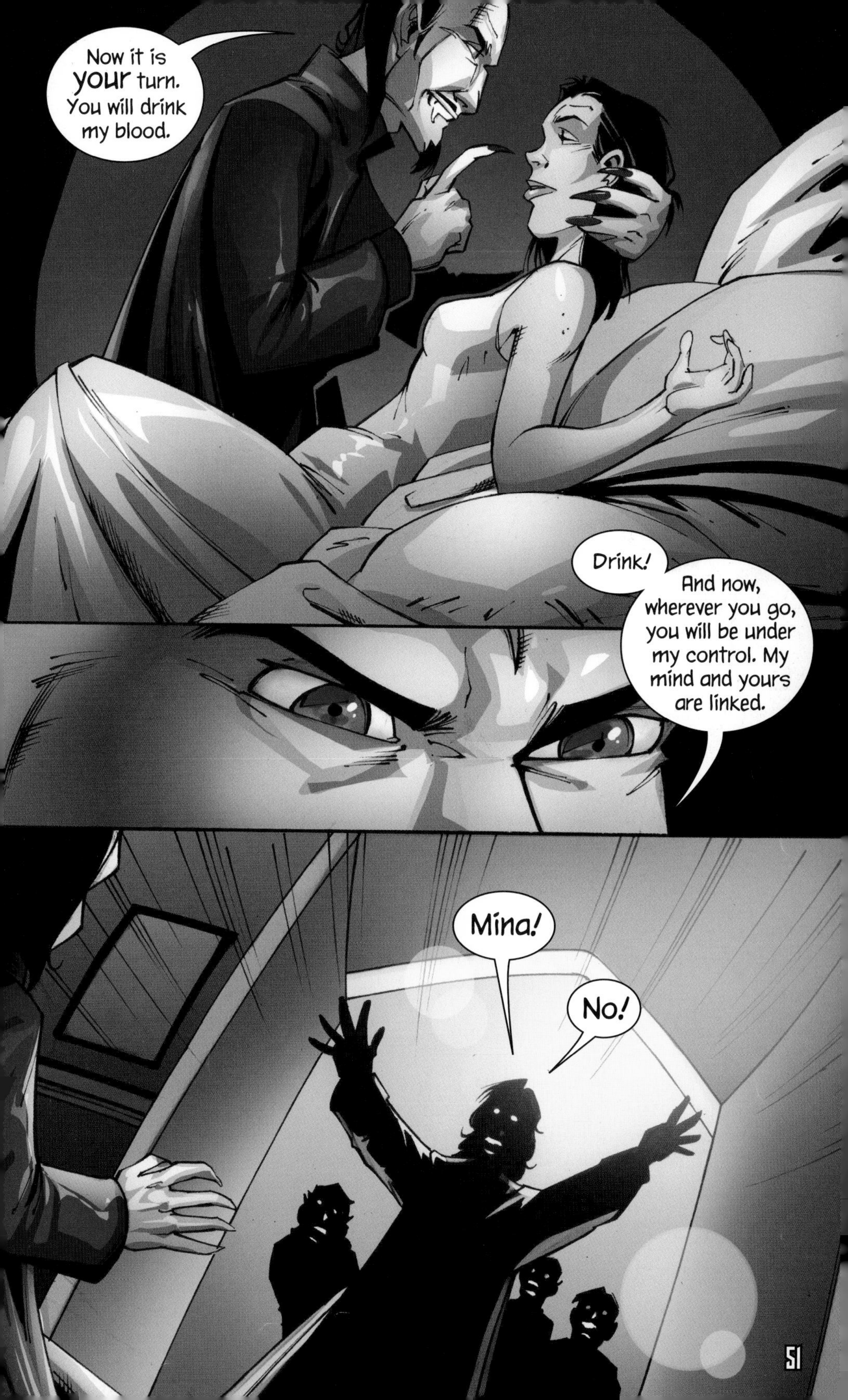
Now it is YOUR turn. You will drink my blood.
Drink!
And now, wherever you go, you will be under my control. My mind and yours are linked.
Mina!
No!

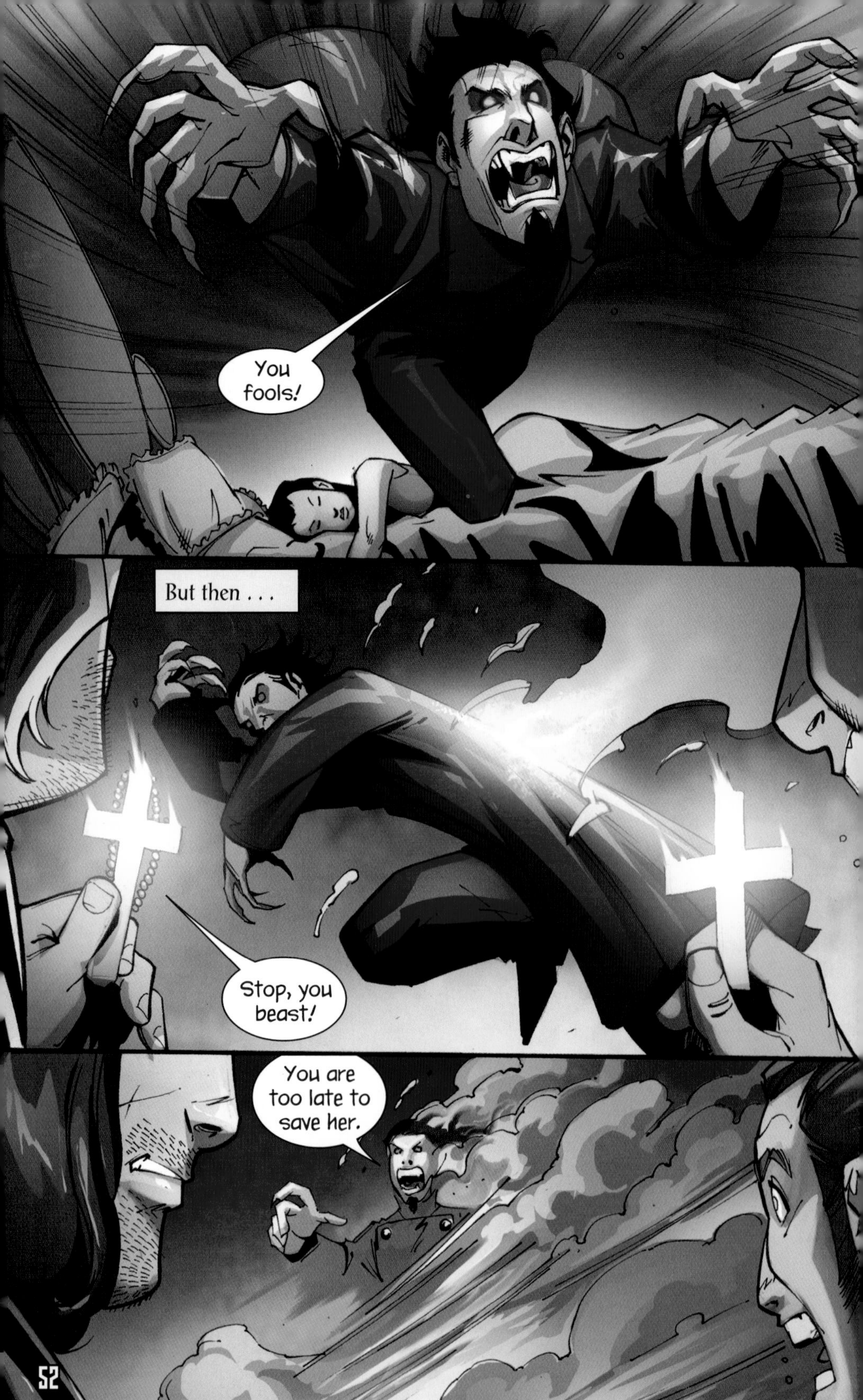
You fools!
But then . . .
Stop, you beast!
You are too late to save her.

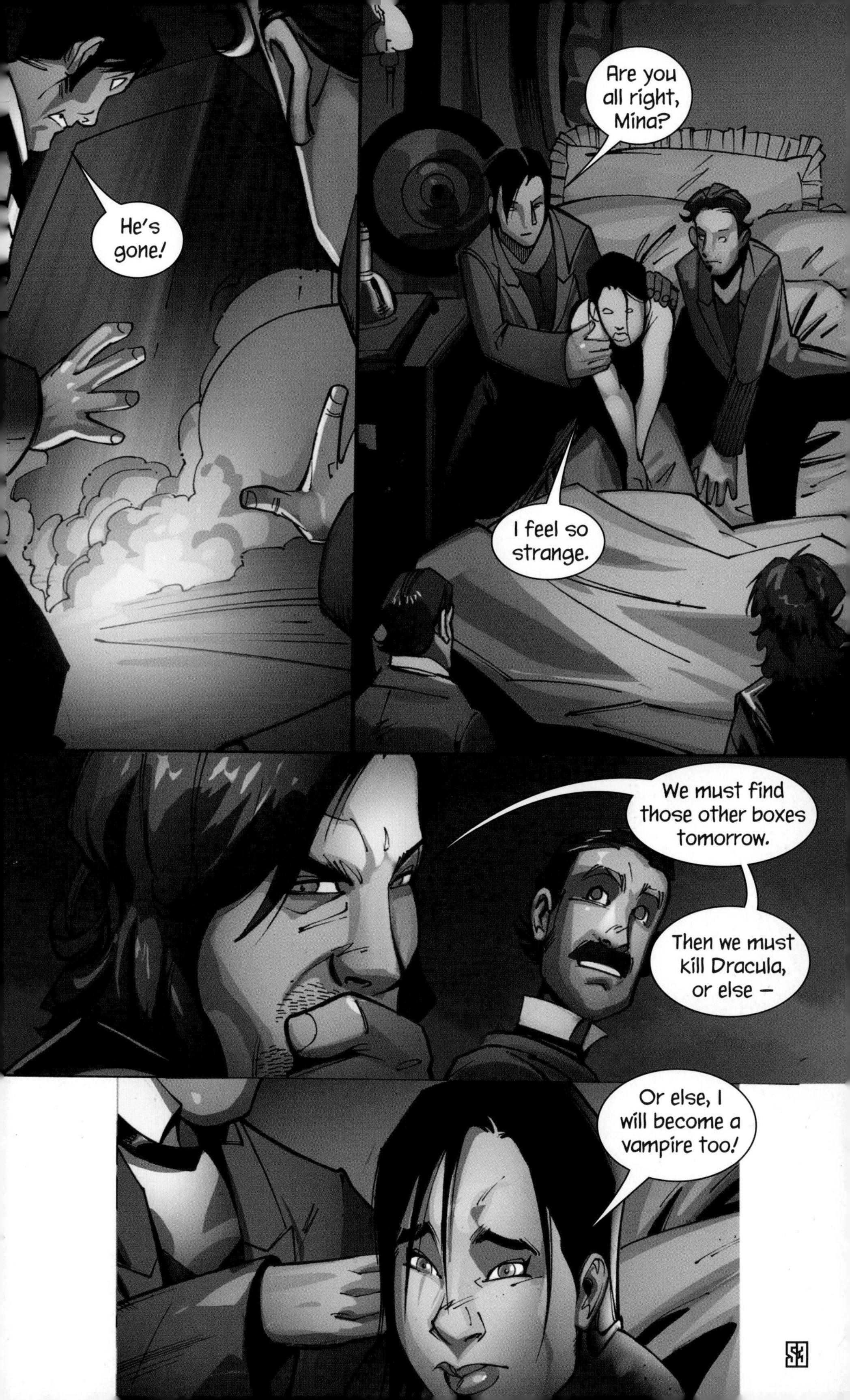
He's gone!
Are you all right, Mina?
I feel so strange.
We must find those other boxes tomorrow.
Then we must kill Dracula, or else —
Or else, I will become a vampire too!

CHAPTER 6: ON THE RUN

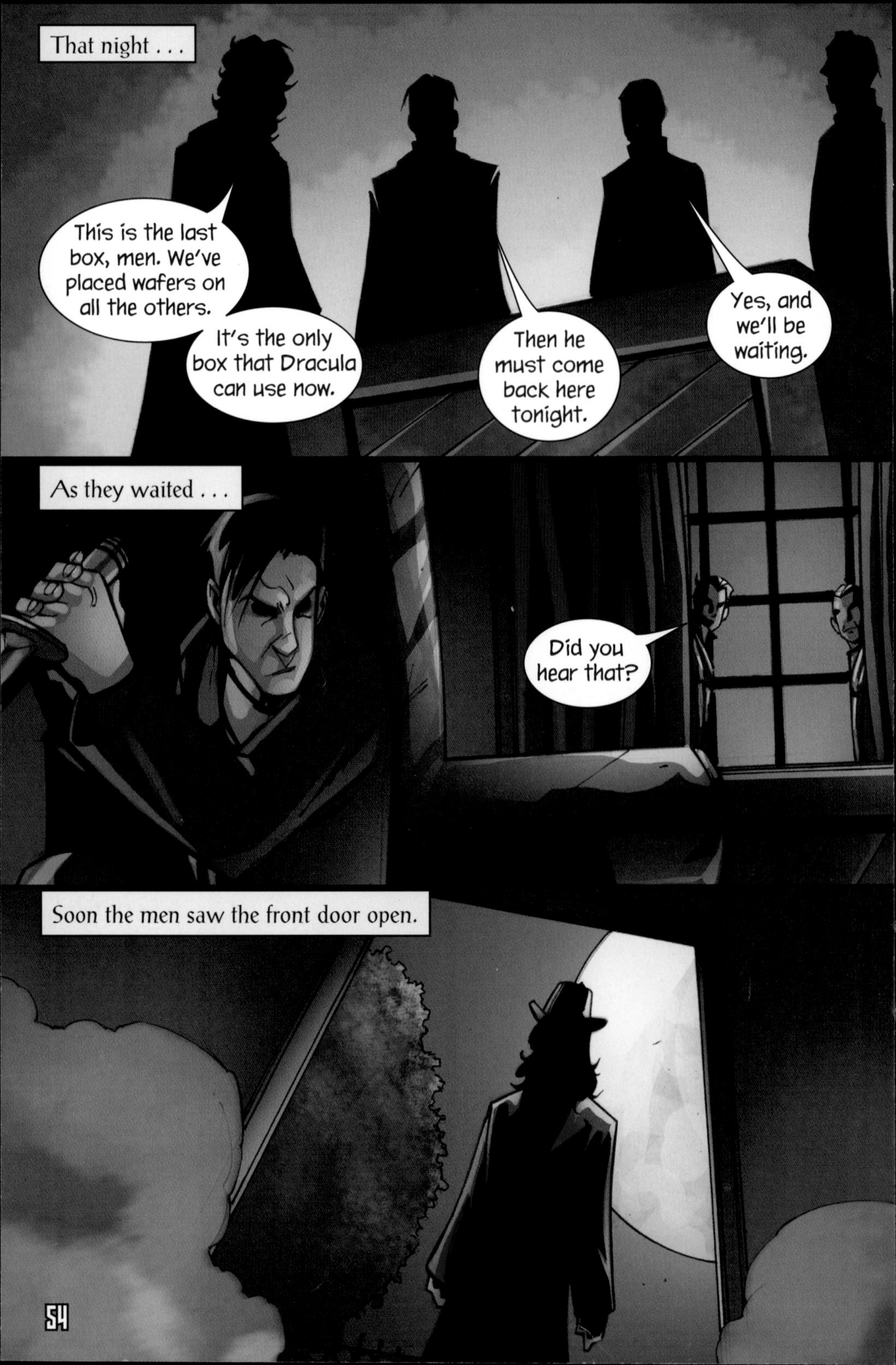
That night . . .
This is the last box, men. We've placed wafers on all the others.
It's the only box that Dracula can use now.
Then he must come back here tonight.
Yes, and we'll be waiting.
As they waited . . .
Did you hear that?
Soon the men saw the front door open.

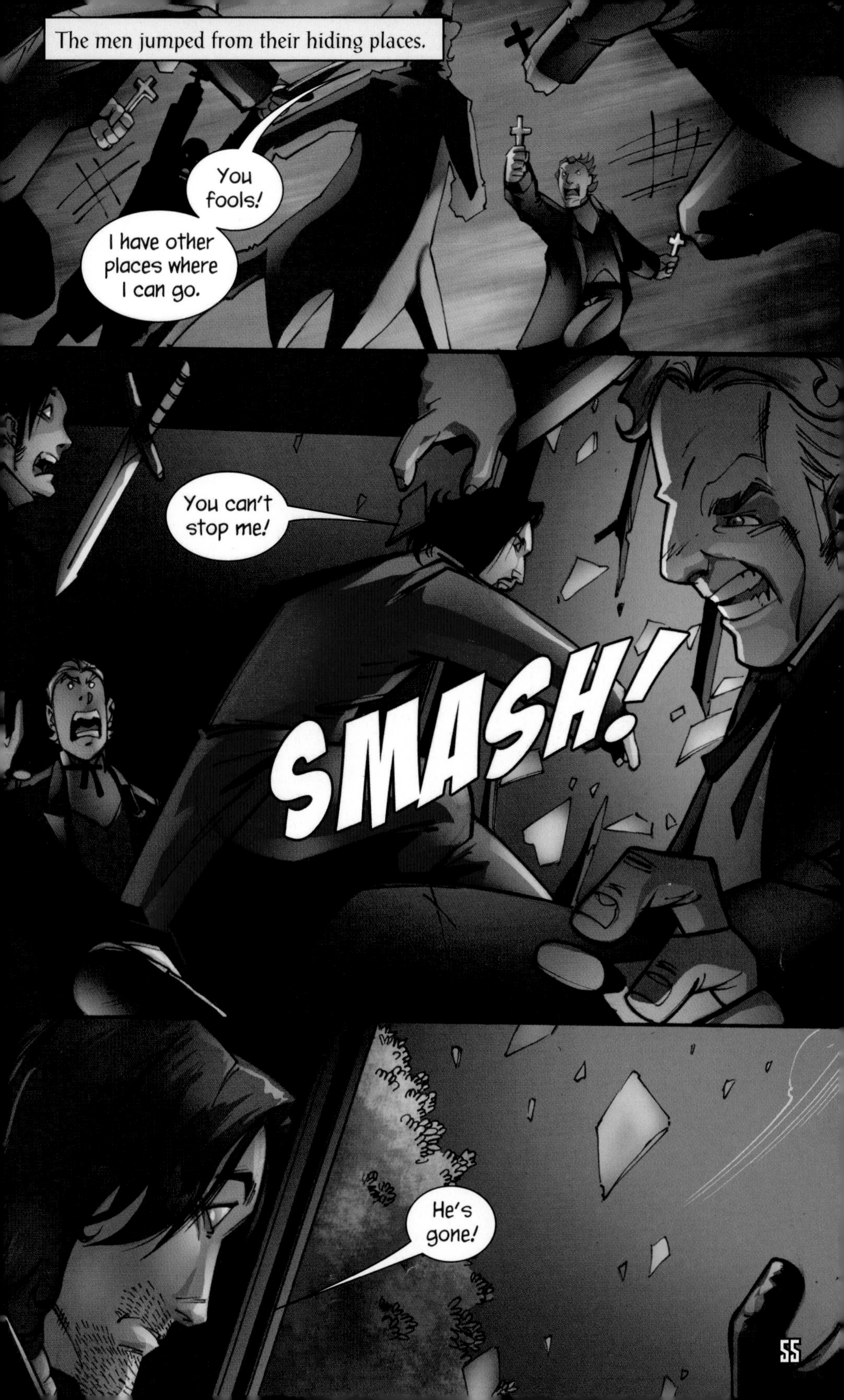
The men jumped from their hiding places.
You fools!
I have other places where I can go.
You can't stop me!
SMASH!
He's gone!

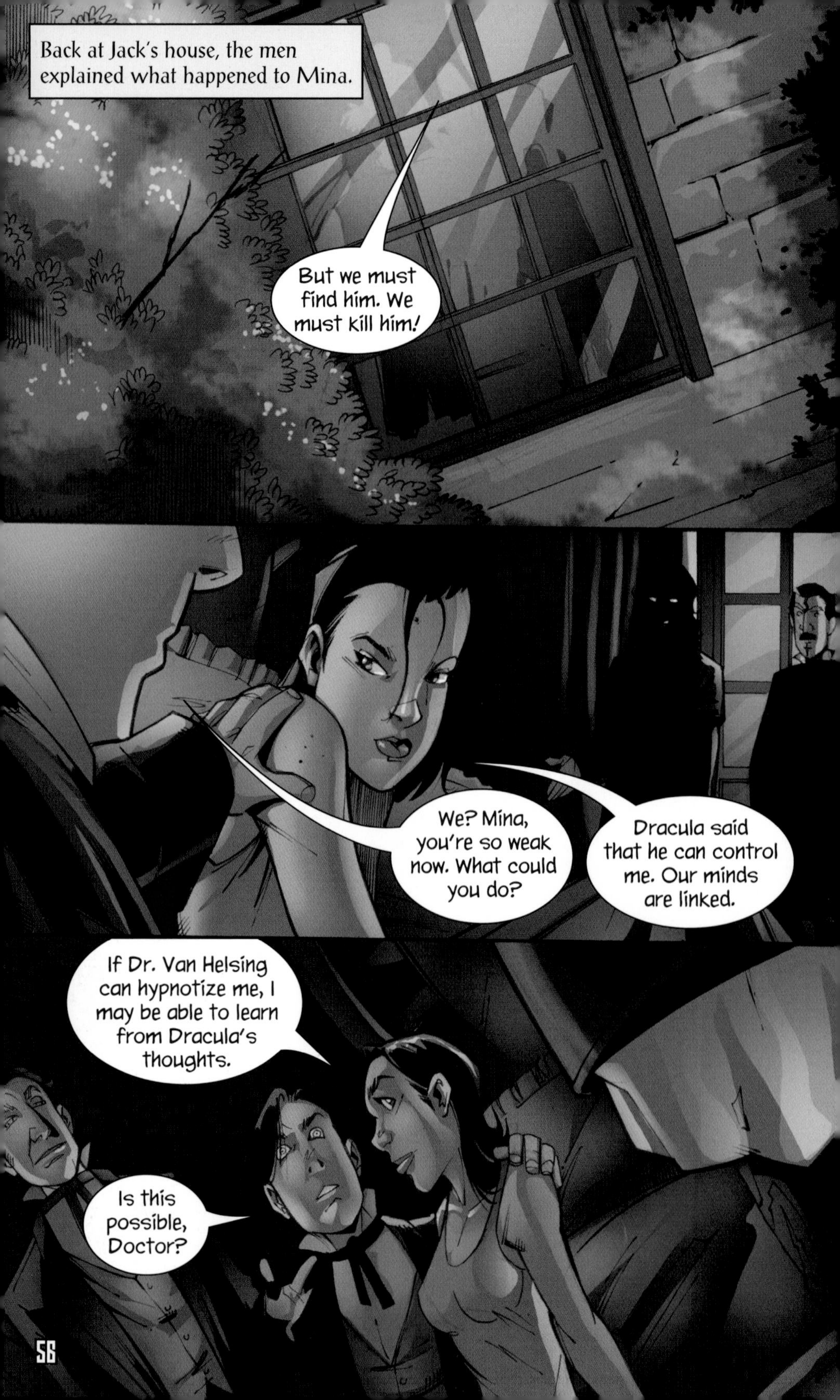

Back at Jack's house, the men explained what happened to Mina.
But we must find him. We must kill him!
We? Mina, you're so weak now. What could you do?
Dracula said that he can control me. Our minds are linked.
If Dr. Van Helsing can hypnotize me, I may be able to learn from Dracula's thoughts.
Is this possible, Doctor?

CHAPTER 7: THE END OF DRACULA

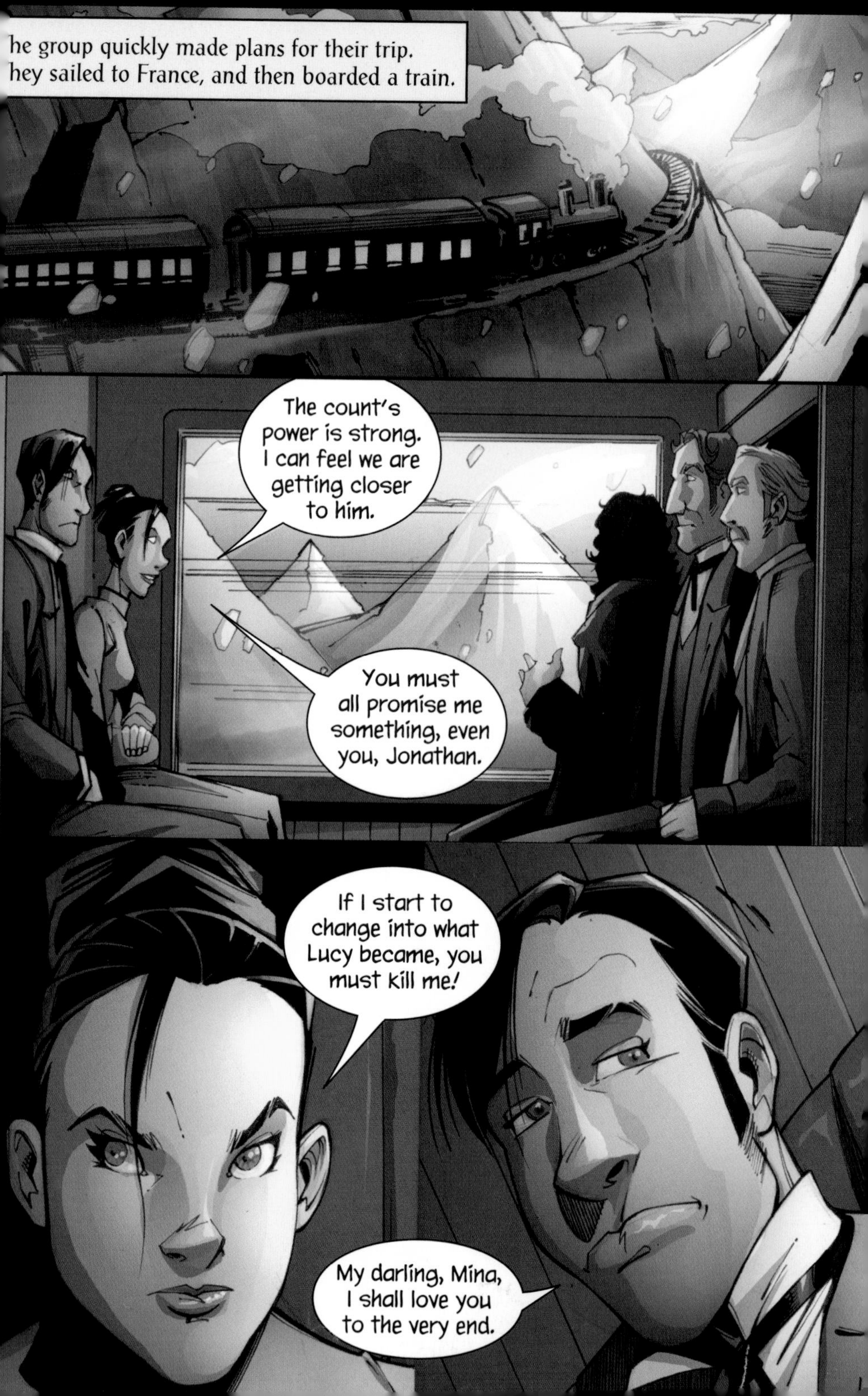
he group quickly made plans for their trip. hey sailed to France, and then boarded a train.
The count's power is strong. I can feel we are getting closer to him.
You must all promise me something, even you, Jonathan.
If I start to change into what Lucy became, you must kill me!
My darling, Mina, I shall love you to the very end.

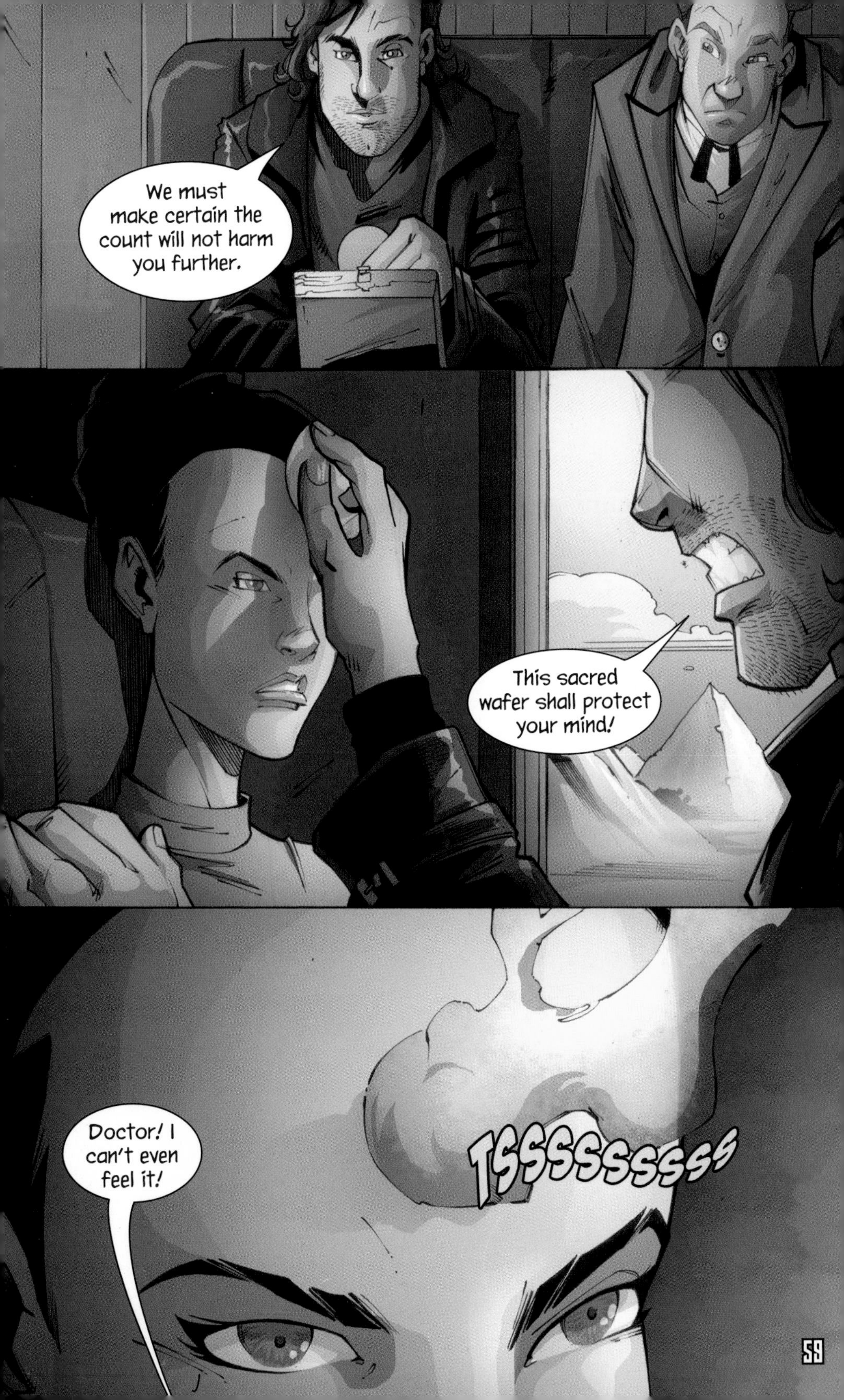
We must make certain the count will not harm you further.
This sacred wafer shall protect your mind!
Doctor! I can't even feel it!
TSSSSSSSSS

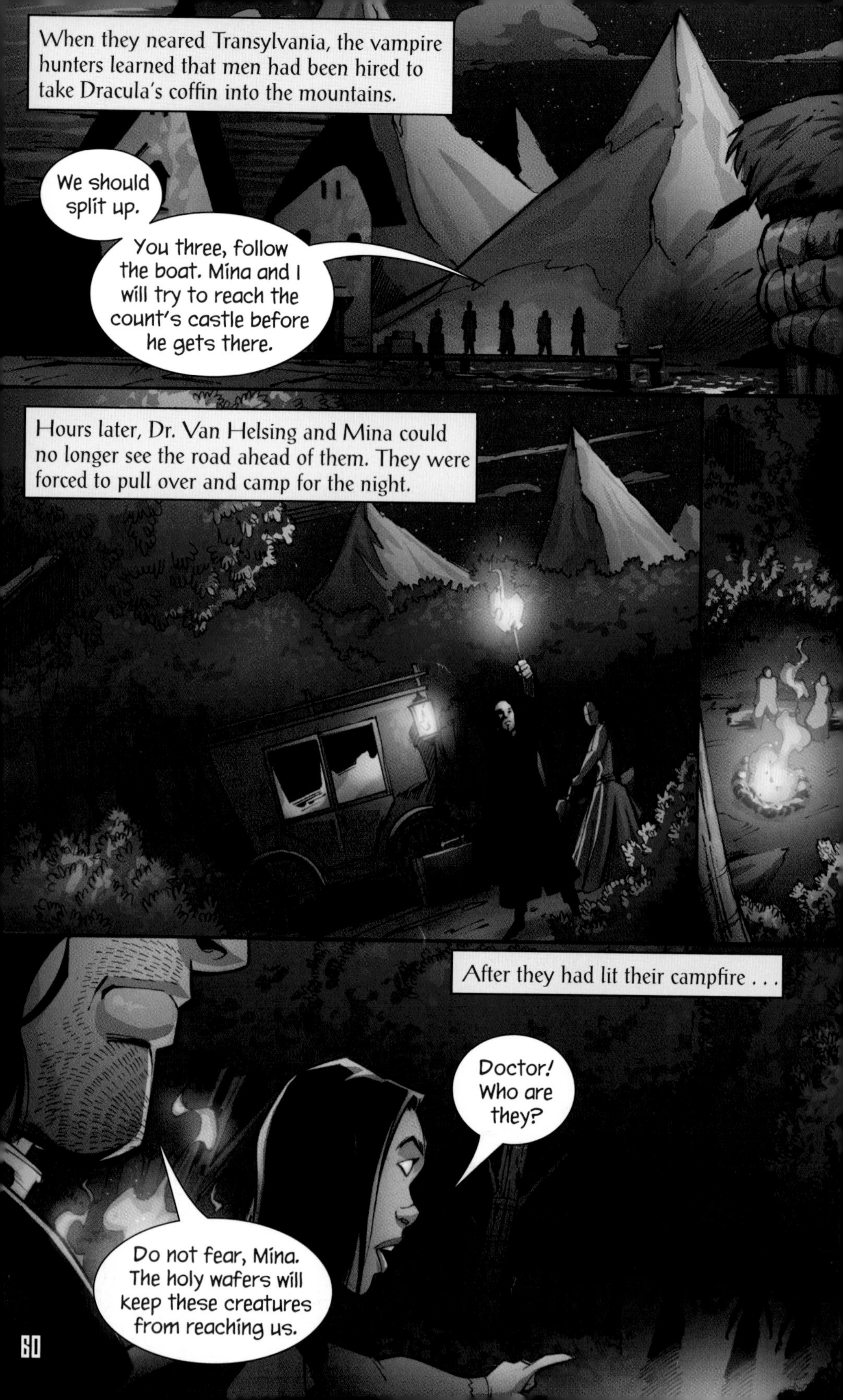

When they neared Transylvania, the vampire hunters learned that men had been hired to take Dracula's coffin into the mountains.
We should split up.
You three, follow the boat. Mina and I will try to reach the count's castle before he gets there.
Hours later, Dr. Van Helsing and Mina could no longer see the road ahead of them. They were forced to pull over and camp for the night.
After they had lit their campfire . . .
Doctor! Who are they?
Do not fear, Mina. The holy wafers will keep these creatures from reaching us.

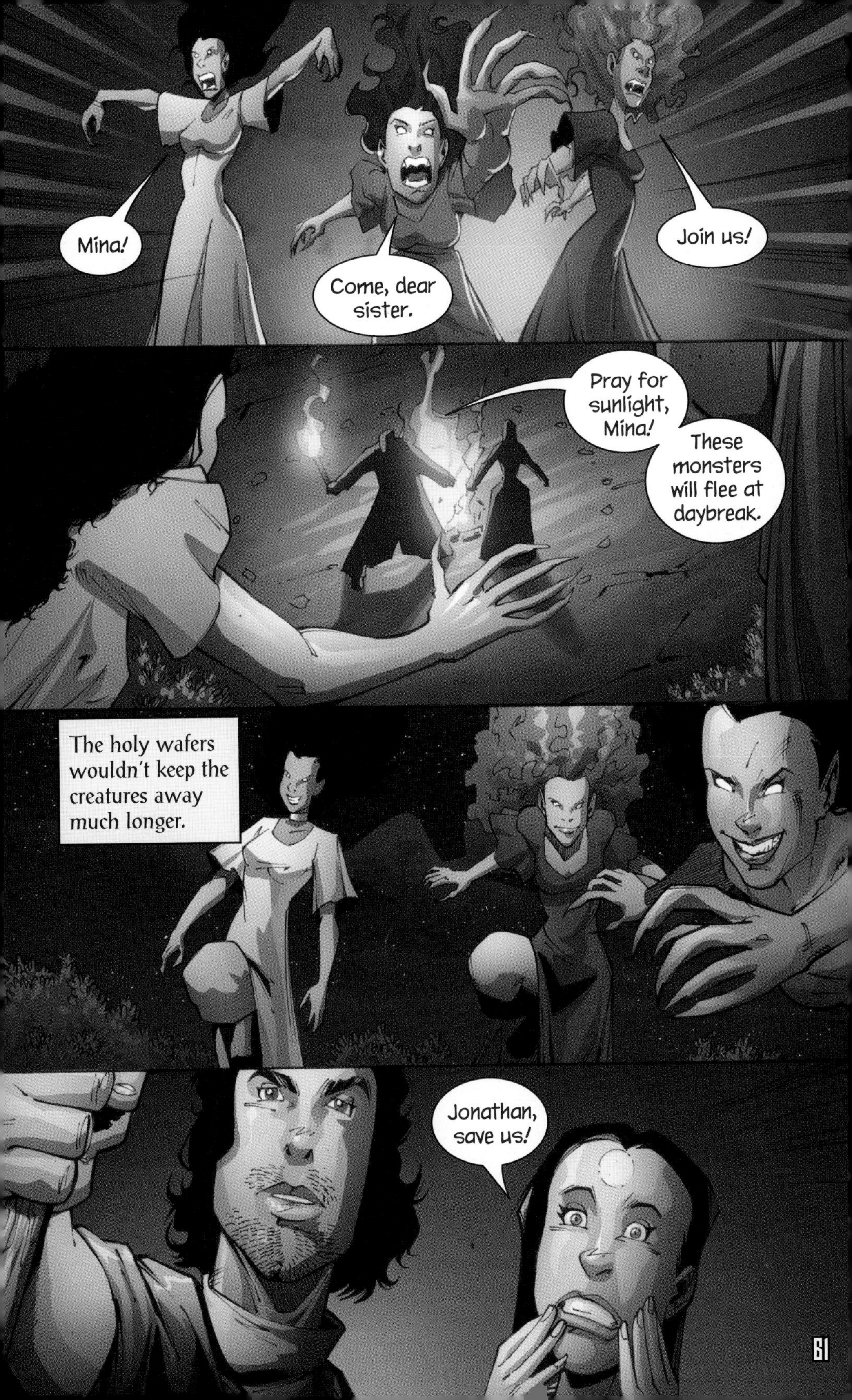
Mina!
Come, dear sister.
Join us!
Pray for sunlight, Mina!
These monsters will flee at daybreak.
The holy wafers wouldn't keep the creatures away much longer.
Jonathan, save us!

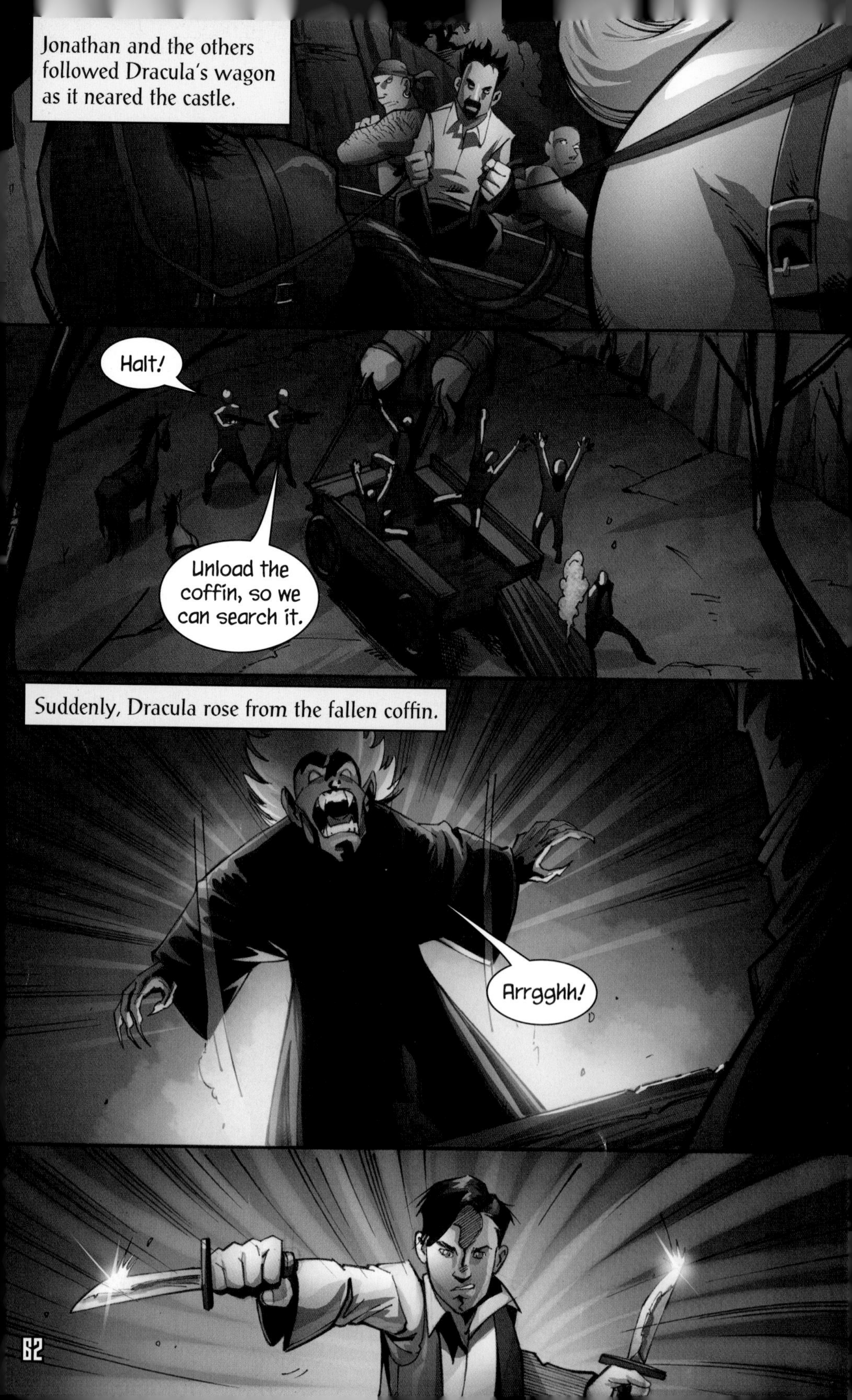
Jonathan and the others followed Dracula's wagon as it neared the castle.
Halt!
Unload the coffin, so we can search it.
Suddenly, Dracula rose from the fallen coffin.
Arrgghh!

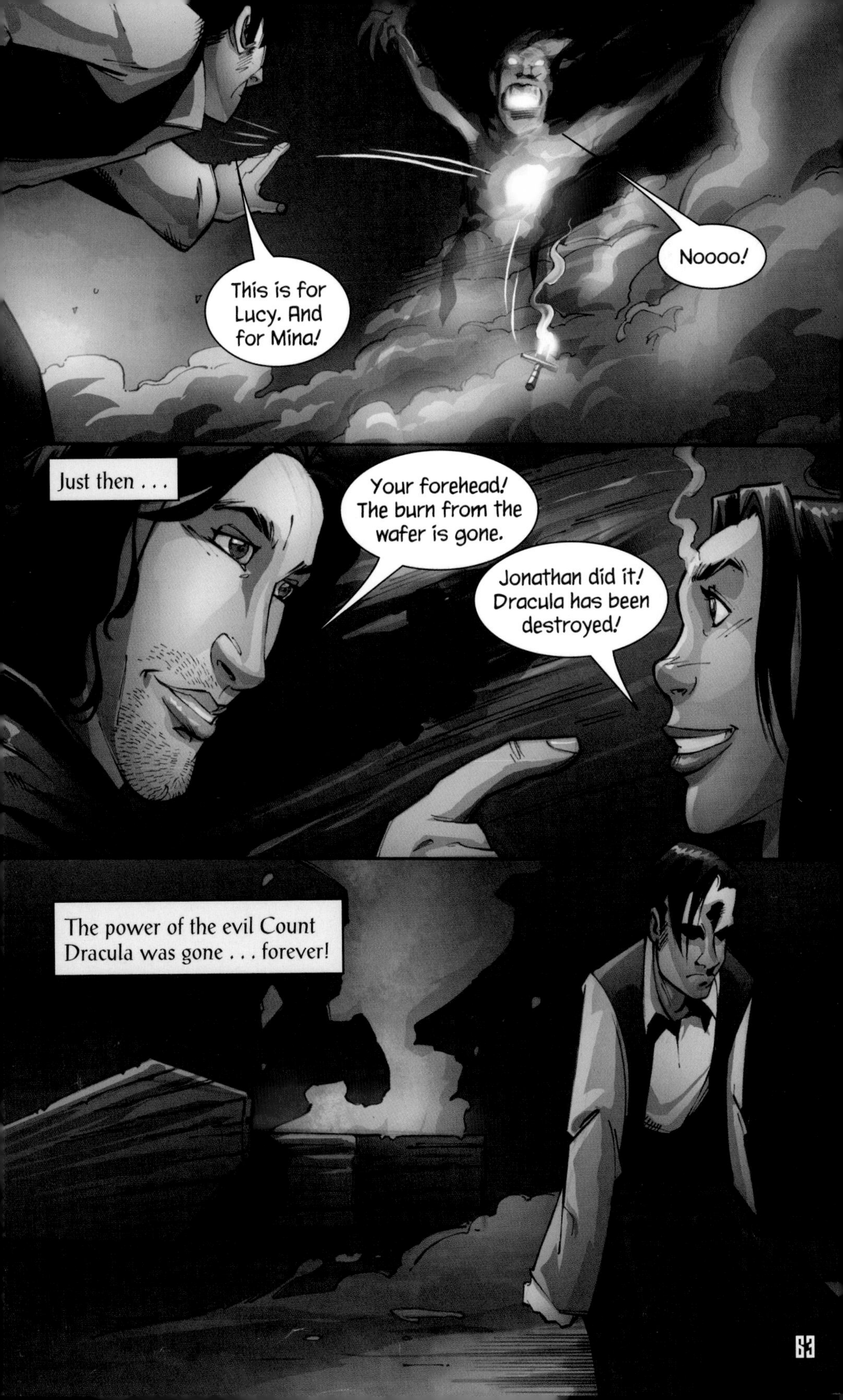

This is for Lucy. And for Mina!
Noooo!
Just then . . .
Your forehead! The burn from the wafer is gone.
Jonathan did it! Dracula has been destroyed!
The power of the evil Count Dracula was gone . . . forever!

ABOUT THE AUTHOR

Bram Stoker was born on November 8, 1847, near Dublin, Ireland. Young Stoker suffered from a mysterious illness. Until age seven, he spent much of his time in bed, reading books and dreaming of becoming a famous writer. After graduating from college, Stoker worked as a civil servant in Dublin Castle but continued to write stories on the side. He had also been interested in vampires and spent several years researching these legends. In 1897, *Dracula* was published. It remains his most famous story, inspiring countless movies, books, TV shows, and Halloween masks.

ABOUT THE RETELLING AUTHOR

Michael Burgan has written more than 90 fiction and nonfiction books for children. A history graduate from the University of Connecticut, Burgan worked at *Weekly Reader* for six years before beginning his freelance career. He has received an award from the Educational Press Association of America and has won several playwriting contests. He lives in Chicago with his wife, Samantha.

GLOSSARY

carriage (KA-rij)—a small vehicle with wheels, often pulled by horses

crucifix (KRU-sih-fiks)—a cross, which Christians believe represents Jesus Christ

curious (KYUR-ee-uhss)—a strong desire to investigate

journal (JUR-nuhl)—a book or notebook where someone records the daily events of his or her life, such as a diary

sacred wafer (SAY-krid WAY-fur)—a round, thin piece of bread often given during a Christian church service

startled (STAR-tuhld)—frightened by being surprised

tomb (TOOM)—a place for holding a dead body

Transylvania (tran-sil-VAIN-yuh)—a real-life mountainous region in eastern Europe

undead (un-DED)—another name for a vampire or zombie

vampire (VAM-pire)—a dead person believed to come out of the grave at night and suck the blood of the living

MORE ABOUT
VAMPIRES

Myths and legends of vampires have haunted people for thousands of years. In fact, author Bram Stoker spent seven years researching the many tales about these creepy creatures for his book.

No one knows who told the first vampire stories, but ancient **Mesopotamians** (meh-soh-puh-TAY-mee-ans) were some of the first. More than 4,000 years ago, these people, from the area of modern-day Iraq, feared an evil goddess called Lamastu. The Mesopotamians believed Lamastu was responsible for many diseases including the death of young children.

Researchers have found tales of blood-sucking creatures all over the world. Most modern legends, however, come from eastern Europe. In fact, many believe the term "vampire" comes from a Russian creature called **Upir** (oo-PEER).

Some myths about vampires are no longer common. For example, eastern Europeans once believed that scattering seeds on the ground could keep vampires away. They thought vampires would stop to count the seeds instead of chasing after their next victim.

Some people believe author Bram Stoker named his character Dracula after a real-life person. In the mid-1400s, Prince Vlad Tepes ruled over what is today Romania. This evil leader was also known as **Vlad Dracula**, meaning "Son of the Dragon."

In the past, some people might have actually returned from the dead! A rare disease called **catalepsy** (KAT-uh-lep-see) can make a person stiff and slow down their breathing. Early doctors sometimes thought these people were dead. When the person eventually woke up, or even escaped from their own grave, they may have been considered a vampire.

Vampire bats are not just found in stories. These winged creatures actually live in parts of Central and South America. They feed on blood from other animals and birds. In fact, vampire bats are the only animals in the world to survive on nothing but blood.

DISCUSSION QUESTIONS

1. In chapter one, Jonathan visits Count Dracula at his castle in Transylvania. Looking back at the story, what clues helped Jonathan realize that the count was a vampire? Do you think he should have figured this out sooner? Why or why not?

2. Do you think the other characters in this story could have stopped Dracula without Dr. Van Helsing? Why or why not? List some of the reasons he was important to the story.

3. What were some of Dracula's powers in this story? What were some of his weaknesses? Were these powers and weaknesses different or similar to other vampire stories that you have read? Explain.

WRITING PROMPTS

1. Throughout history, thousands of stories have been written about Dracula and other vampires. Now try to write your own! What will your vampires look like? Who will they haunt? How will your characters stop them?

2. Do you have a favorite scary story? Write it down and share it with your friends and family.

3. In this story, Dracula can turn into a bat and a wolf. If you had the power to turn into any animal, what animal would it be and why? Write about what your adventures as that animal would be like.

OTHER BOOKS

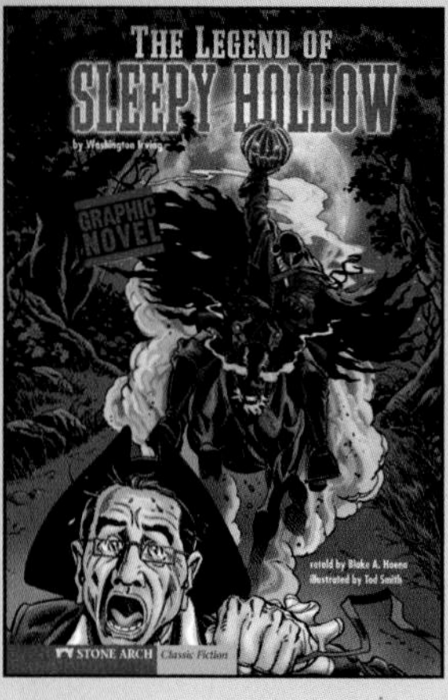
THE LEGEND OF
SLEEPY HOLLOW
GRAPHIC NOVEL
STONE ARCH Classic Fiction

Sleepy Hollow

A headless horseman haunts Sleepy Hollow! At least that's the legend in the tiny village of Tarrytown. But scary stories won't stop the town's new schoolmaster, Ichabod Crane, from crossing through the hollow, especially when the beautiful Katrina Balt lives on the other side. Will Ichabod win over his beloved or discover that the legend of Sleepy Hollow is actually true?

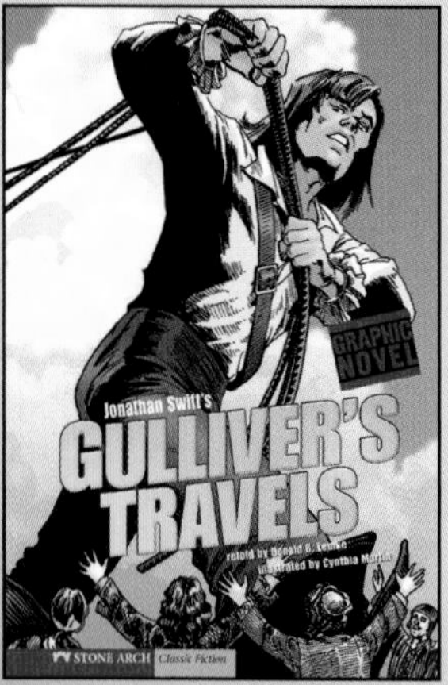
GRAPHIC NOVEL
Jonathan Swift's
GULLIVER'S TRAVELS
STONE ARCH Classic Fiction

Gulliver's Travels

Lemuel Gulliver always dreamed of sailing across seas, but he never could have imagined the places his travels would take him. On the island of Lilliput, he is captured by tiny creatures no more than six inches tall. In a country of Blefuscu, he is nearly squashed by an army of giants. His adventures could be the greatest tales ever told, if he survives long enough to tell them.

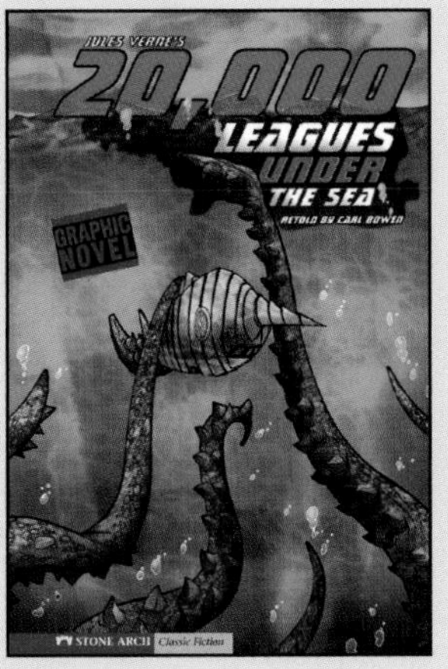
JULES VERNE'S
20,000
LEAGUES
UNDER
THE SEA
GRAPHIC NOVEL
STONE ARCH Classic Fiction

20,000 Leagues Under the Sea

Scientist Pierre Aronnax and his trusty servant set sail to hunt a sea monster. With help from Ned Land, the world's greatest harpooner, the men soon discover that the creature is really a high-tech submarine. To keep this secret from being revealed, the sub's leader, Captain Nemo, takes the men hostage. Now, each man must decide whether to trust Nemo or try to escape this underwater world.

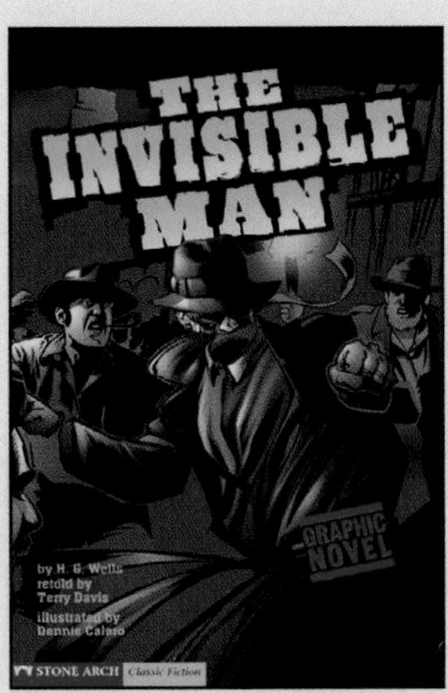
THE
INVISIBLE
MAN
GRAPHIC NOVEL
by H. G. Wells
retold by
Terry Davis
STONE ARCH Classic Fiction

The Invisible Man

Late one night, a mysterious man wanders into a tiny English village. He is covered from head to toe in bandages. After a series of burglaries, the villagers grow suspicious. Who is this man? Where did he come from? When the villagers attempt to arrest the stranger, he suddenly reveals his secret—he is invisible! How can anyone stop the Invisible Man?

INTERNET SITES

Do you want to know more about subjects related to this book? Or are you interested in learning about other topics? Then check out FactHound, a fun, easy way to find Internet sites.

Our investigative staff has already sniffed out great sites for you!

Here's how to use FactHound:

1. Visit www.facthound.com

2. Select your grade level.

3. To learn more about subjects related to this book, type in the book's ISBN number: **9781434204486**.

4. Click the **Fetch It** button.

FactHound will fetch the best Internet sites for you!